黃金口說

那于 著

托福800單字

TOEFL 800 WORDS

從苦背單字到流利口說對話
托福口說實用單字大公開

突破學習的自我設限，在短時間內大幅提升英文單字量
有效提升背誦英文單字的效率

熟悉掌握常見單字的詞義和使用方法
學習的本質是記憶，而記憶的本質是重複
投入時間是學習英文的必經之路

目錄

前言

無論你是否要考托福，這些單字你都要會

有人可能會問，市面上的托福單字書已經數不勝數，這本書究竟有何特別的價值和意義？

為了客觀且充分地回答這個問題，我把可能會讀到這本書的同學分成兩類，你可以看看自己屬於其中的哪類。

第一類，還不確定自己是不是要考托福的同學。對於這類同學，即使你不去背誦全部的托福單字（因為你還沒有下定決心要考托福），你也有必要背誦並學習這些單字。作為托福考試的一部分，托福口說考驗的是全面的英語能力。托福口說單字涉及日常表達、校園對話，以及北美大學課堂的真實情景，因此這些單字都是十分重要且實用的。「重要」是因為這些單字的熟悉與否直接決定你是否能聽懂並了解英文內容，「實用」是因為這些單字會大量地出現在你未來的生活中。

所以，即使你還沒有確定要考托福，背誦這 800 個單字也能提升你的英語口說能力。

第二類，已經確定自己一定會去考托福，甚至已經開始學習或上課的同學。托福口說是學生分數最低的考試項目。有很

多同學可以在閱讀和聽力部分取得幾乎滿分，口說卻只有尷尬的 20 分左右（滿分為 30 分），導致總分不夠漂亮，申請的學校也不如預期。根據我自己將近十年的托福學習和教學經驗，學生在考試中總是不能克服以下幾點，導致無法獲得較高的分數。第一，看不懂、聽不懂原文；第二，看懂、聽懂之後，記不起來；第三，看懂、聽懂、記起來之後，說不出口。

而以下這三點就是本書要解決的問題。

第一，為了更快速地看懂、聽懂，我們只背重要單字。

本書中的 800 個單字來自將近 50 回托福考古題，且出現頻率在 3 次以上。在收錄單字的過程中，我們刪除了那些多次出現，但只出現在一回考古題中的單字，且不收錄不影響了解題目的人名、地名，以及奇怪的動植物名，如 Warren、Whitney、wrasse 和 cactus 等等。本書只收錄了很有可能直接出現在考題中的重要單字，讓準備考試事半功倍。

第二，對詞義的了解程度決定了看懂、聽懂的速度。

與其他的單字書不同，本書並未提供每個單字的全部解釋，只提供在托福口說中真正會考到的解釋。每個單字通常只有一個最主要的解釋。我們相信「Less is more」。記住一個單字在考試中最主要的解釋，可以提升準備考試的效率。同時，只有將一個單字的主要解釋融會貫通，再去記得其他解釋，才不會出現混淆和遺忘。所以，為了提升看懂、聽懂的速度，我們

需要熟悉單字的主要解釋。

第三，記得必要的類似詞彙，讓溝通更流利。

很多同學在回答口說題目的時候，會出現吃螺絲、忘記單字等現象，明明剛剛聽到的單字，轉眼間就說不出來了。這是因為單字量不夠，在忘記一個單字的時候，沒有辦法快速想到一個類似詞彙來替代。所以，本書針對托福口說，列出了所有與單字主要解釋類似的詞彙提供考生參考，進而大大降低「想不起來單字」這種現象出現的可能性。透過記得必要的類似詞彙，提升表達的流暢度和穩定性。

因此，不管你要不要報考托福，這些單字都要融會貫通，因為這些都是你在日常生活中會頻繁使用的單字。如果已經確定了要報考托福，你要了解到托福口說是真正拉開分數，決定你是「考過了」還是「考得好」的主要項目。能否盡快熟悉這些單字，更會直接影響你的考試結果。

所以，這本書會以它獨特的價值和意義，協助你準備托福口說，並提升英語口說能力。

本書使用方法

　　首先，必須先澄清一個概念：對於背單字而言，方法沒那麼重要。但其實背單字的本質就是記憶，而記憶的本質是重複。「記憶技巧」或許會讓記憶的效率有所改善，但重複的次數、投入的時間，永遠是記憶並熟悉單字的必經之路。

　　試想，當你因為厭倦了「從 A 到 Z」的單字排列而無法記下所有單字時，難道換成「從 Z 到 A」或者「隨機排列」就能快速地記下所有單字嗎？因此，我們要有「Back to the basic」的能力，要有看透事物本質的思考方式。我們還要了解到，有時實現目標靠的不僅是方法、技巧，而且還有勤奮、努力。背單字，也是如此。

　　為了幫助大家高效率地使用本書，並在最短時間內提升單字記憶的效果，我想分享以下五點方法和建議。

一、短時間集中突破

　　根據記憶心理學家的研究結果，正常情況下每個人每天可以背 30 個新單字，而在有強大意志力的幫助下，最多可以背大約 60 個新單字。而我們建議大家每天背 90 個本書中的單字，

且本書收錄的單字均有附上衍生詞彙、類似詞彙和例句，能夠幫助大家提高效率。

每天背 90 個新單字看似不可能，實際上並沒有那麼困難。如果每天背 90 個新單字，8 天可以背完本書；如果每天背 30 個新單字，24 天才能完成。

無論做任何事情，努力往往最重要。突破自己的精神也將成為你終身受用的精神財富。

▌二、背誦結合聽力

托福口說包含閱讀和聽力，這代表我們不僅要能夠讀懂，還要能夠聽懂。這代表著，我們需要在聽到單字的同時，能夠想到單字解釋，並快速了解，進而順利作答。

因此，大家在背單字的過程中一定要重視「聽力」的訓練。對於發音不確定或者自認為有難度的單字，一定要仔細聽單字的發音，並且跟著一起唸直到熟記。

▌三、讀懂考古題例句

本書中收錄的單字均有附上托福口說的考古題例句。大家一定要讀懂例句，掌握單字在考古題中的詞義和用法。

四、背誦類似解釋的單字

很多時候，大家在回答題目時會出現不順的現象。這是因為突然忘記了要說什麼，或者忘記了單字的解釋。而解決這個問題的有效辦法就是，記得足夠數量的類似詞彙。

例如，當我們想表達「敏銳的」的時候，如果我們忘記了「acute」，我們可以用「pointedly」或「sharply」來表達。背了越多的類似解釋的單字，越能夠提升表達的流暢度。

五、檢測背單字的成果

背誦單字之後，檢測成果的環節不可或缺。但是，與很多單字書不同，我們並沒有在每個單字表之後設計練習題。對於口說來講，在理解的前提下說出單字，才是最有效、最有意義的練習。大家可以遵循以下步驟來檢測自己的背單字的效果：

第一步，看英文單字，並在 1 至 2 秒內想到對應的中文解釋；第二步，看中文解釋，並在 1 至 2 秒內想到對應的英文單字；第三步，聽單字的英文發音，並在 1 至 2 秒內想到對應的英文單字。完成這三步，大家對單字的掌握和理解應該會比較熟悉了。

本書體例說明

　　本書收錄的皆為托福口說中的常見的詞彙，可以作為高效率了解並回答托福口說題目的基礎。全書的體例編排如下：

一、單字

　　本書僅收錄托福口說考古題中的常見的主要單字，並已排除了不影響理解的專業單字以及不影響表達的單字，以減輕大家準備考試的負擔。

二、音標

　　為了更好地幫助大家聽懂並了解托福口說中的美式發音，本書普遍使用 KK 音標，如單字「component」的音標是 [kəmˈpoʊnənt]。

三、中文釋義

　　每個單字皆有其重要的解釋和詞性。

四、類似詞彙

針對每一個可能會有表達困難的單字，本書列出了與其主要解釋相近的詞彙。這樣讓大家能透過類似詞彙更好地記憶單字解釋，當大家在遇到表達上的困難或者不順時，可以透過類似詞彙快速替代表達，從而更加流暢地作答。

五、衍生詞彙

托福口說考古題中的常見單字和主要解釋一直在不斷變化。在列出全部主要單字的同時，我們收錄了重點單字的衍生詞彙，讓大家準備得更加齊全，以利面對口說考試。

六、考古題例句

本書收錄的所有單字皆有附上托福口說考古題例句。大家可以觀察單字在例句中的用法，更仔細地了解托福口說的難度、風格。不僅讓自己的口說能力更上一層樓，而且對托福考試的其他項目也有幫助。

單字表 1

▶ **ability** [ə'bɪlətɪ]

【釋】 *n.* 能力

【例】 But what I wanna talk about now is a special *ability* some fish have.

【衍】 able *adj.* 有能力的

【近】 capacity

▶ **abiotic** [ˌebaɪ'ɑtɪk]

【釋】 *adj.* 非生物的

【例】 Biotic and *abiotic* factors cause continual changes in the number of individuals that make up a population of organisms.

【衍】 abiochemistry *n.* 無機化學

【近】 dead, nonliving

▶ **abruptly** [ə'brʌptlɪ]

【釋】 *adv.* 突然地

【例】 To create contrast, color contrast, you need to *abruptly* change your color scheme once in a while.

【衍】 abruptness *n.* 突然；唐突

【近】 suddenly

▶ **absence** ['æbsns]

【釋】 *n.* 缺乏

【例】 So product reliability means, basically, the *absence* of defects or problems that you weren't expecting.

【衍】 absent *adj.* 不在場的；心不在焉的

【近】 shortage

▶ **absorb** [əb'zɔrb]

【釋】 *v.* 吸收

【例】 So the frogs are able to *absorb* and store moisture during wet rainy times which they can rely on to get through dry periods.

【衍】 absorption *n.* 吸 收 ； 全神貫注

【近】 attract, engage

▶ accessible [əkˈsɛsəbl]

【釋】 *adj.* 平易近人的

【例】 But then they became much more *accessible*.

【衍】 accessibility *n.* 易接近

【近】 accostable

▶ accessory [əkˈsɛsərɪ]

【釋】 *n.* 配件

【例】 Now how does this company make profits with its low-priced computers? Well, one thing that's often done is to encourage their customers to buy *accessories* also manufactured by them, like printers or software.

【衍】 accessorial *adj.* 附 屬 的 ； 額外的

【近】 attachment

▶ accommodate [əˈkɑməˌdet]

【釋】 *v.* 容納

【例】 If the building were open more hours, though, it would be easier to *accommodate* the large number of students who want to reserve rooms.

【衍】 accommodation *n.* 住處 ； 調節

【近】 adapt, contain

▶ account [ə'kaunt]

【釋 1】 *n.* 帳號

【例】 People mentally store some money in one *account* to be saved, while they imagine other money being stored in another account from which money can be taken and freely spent.

【衍】 accountant *n.* 會計 accountable *adj.* 有責任的

【釋 2】 *n.* 考慮

【例】 People take each other into *account* in their daily behavior and in fact, the very presence of others can affect behavior.

▶ accurate ['ækjərət]

【釋】 *adj.* 準確的

【例】 One objective of any experiment is, of course, to obtain *accurate* results.

【衍】 accurately *adv.* 精確地

【近】 precise

▶ accustom [ə'kʌstəm]

【釋】 *v.* 使……習慣

【例】 At first, people are not *accustomed* to the new technology and may not understand it; they may therefore have a negative attitude toward it.

【衍】 accustomization *n.* 適應 accustomed *adj.* 習慣的

【近】 habituate

▶ achieve [ə'tʃiv]

【釋】 *v.* 實現

【例】 Insect swarms are able to accomplish tasks that individual insects would not be able to *achieve*.

【衍】 achievement *n.* 成就

【近】 accomplish

▶ acquire [ə'kwaɪr]

【釋】 *v.* 獲得

【例】 They could *acquire* silk.

【衍】 acquirement *n.* 取得；成就

【近】 earn

▶ acupuncture ['ækjupʌŋktʃɚ]

【釋】 *n.* 針灸

【例】 For instance, many people in the US have accepted the practice of *acupuncture*.

【衍】 acupuncturist *n.* 針灸醫生

【近】 needling, pinprick

▶ acute [ə'kjut]

【釋】 *adj.* 敏銳的

【例】 Another important adaptation of many sea birds is an *acute*, highly developed sense of smell.

【衍】 acutely *adv.* 尖 銳 地； 劇烈地

【近】 pointed, sharp

▶ adaptation [ˌædæp'teʃən]

【釋】 *n.* 適應

【例】 Another helpful *adaptation* in some deep-sea organisms is the ability to generate light.

【衍】 adapt *v.* 適應；改編 adaptive *adj.* 適應的；適合的

【近】 orientation

▶ **additional** [ə'dɪʃənl]

【釋】 *adj.* 額外的

【例】 The university has announced that it will charge a small *additional* fee for these dinners in order to pay for the special gourmet food ingredients that will be required.

【衍】 addition *n.* 新增 additive *adj.* 附加的 *n.* 添加劑

【近】 attached, added

▶ **administrator** [əd'mɪnɪstretɚ]

【釋】 *n.* 管理員

【例】 When asked to explain the decline in enrollments, the *administrator* pointed to the fact that most evening classes are taught by teaching assistants, who are usually graduate students.

【衍】 administrate *v.* 管理；經營 administration *n.* 管理

【近】 supervisor, conductor

▶ **admission** [əd'mɪʃən]

【釋】 *n.* 入學

【例】 The staff of the *admissions* office no longer have time to lead the campus tours.

【衍】 admissible *adj.* 可容許的；可採納的

▶ **admit** [əd'mɪt]

【釋】 *v.* 承認

【例】 She just came right out and *admitted* to the audience that they cost a lot more than most other companies' pots and pans.

【衍】 admittance *n.* 進入；通道

【近】 accept, recognize

▶ adult [ə'dʌlt]

【釋】 *adj.* 成年的

【例】 For example, *adult* ants normally like to eat things that are rich in sugar.

【衍】 adulthood *n.* 成年（期）

【近】 grown, mature

▶ aerial ['ɛrɪəl]

【釋】 *adj.* 空中的

【例】 Attached to the tree, sometimes 30 or 40 meters high, these *aerial* plants have access to sunlight but not to nutrients from the soil below.

【衍】 aeriality *n.* 空虛 aeration *n.* 通風

▶ affordable [ə'fɔrdəbl]

【釋】 *adj.* 實惠的

【例】 So what did they do? Well, they offered a computer at an *affordable* price, lower than existing brands.

【衍】 afford *v.* 給予；提供；買得起

【近】 inexpensive

▶ agenda [ə'dʒɛndə]

【釋】 *n.* 議程

【例】 Someone sets an *agenda* in advance, emails it to everyone before the meeting, and then makes sure when you meet that you stay focused on your goals.

▶ agonistic [ˌægəˈnɪstɪk]

【釋】 *adj.* 格鬥的

【例】 To resolve these conflicts, two animals of the same species may engage in *agonistic* behavior.

【衍】 agonist *n.* 激動劑；興奮劑

【近】 aggressive, battlesome

▶ ailment [ˈelmənt]

【釋】 *n.* 小病

【例】 The situation at the health center is unacceptable: you sit in a crowded waiting room for hours waiting to get treatment for minor *ailments*.

【衍】 ail *v.* 生病；使困擾 *n.* 病痛 ailing *adj.* 生病的

▶ altitude [ˈæltəˌtud]

【釋】 *n.* 高度

【例】 On the other hand, if the bird carried the shellfish up to a higher *altitude*, an altitude higher than is necessary to crack the shell, it'd be wasting energy.

【近】 height

▶ alumni [əˈlʌmnaɪ]

【釋】 *n.* 校友

【例】 It's true that we do have a lot of very generous *alumni*.

【衍】 alumnus *n.* 男校友 alumna *n.* 女校友

▶ ancient [ˈenʃənt]

【釋】 *adj.* 古代的

【例】 So, most cities of the *an-*

cient world tended to be small, often limited to the banks of a river.

【近】 old

▶ **announcement** [əˈnaunsmənt]

【釋】 *n.* 公告

【例】 But maybe you could ask the French department to port the *announcement* on its website.

【衍】 announce *v.* 宣布；播報 announcer *n.* 廣播員

【近】 declaration

▶ **anonymous** [əˈnɑnəməs]

【釋】 *adj.* 匿名的

【例】 You didn't know? An *anonymous* donor is paying the bill for most of the sculpture.

【衍】 anonymization *n.* 匿名化

【近】 faceless, innominate

▶ **anthropology** [ˌænθrəˈpɑlədʒɪ]

【釋】 *n.* 人類學

【例】 Well, you know how I'm president of the *anthropology* club... well... I'm supposed to drive everyone in the club to see a special exhibit at the museum tomorrow.

【衍】 anthropologist *n.* 人類學家 anthropologic *adj.* 人類學的

【近】 humanics

▶ **anxious** [ˈæŋkʃəs]

【釋】 *adj.* 焦慮的

【例】 This constant state of dependency can make kids feel uneasy and *anxious*.

【衍】 anxiety *n.* 焦慮；渴望 anxiously *adv.* 不安地

▶ appeal [ə'pil]

【釋】 *v.* 吸引

【例】 So, let's talk about a couple of ways product containers can be designed to *appeal* to consumers.

【衍】 appealing *adj.* 吸引人的

【近】 attract

▶ appearance [ə'pɪrəns]

【釋】 *n.* 外觀

【例】 Another important design goal is to give the container a pleasing *appearance* so that consumers will feel

comfortable displaying it in their homes.

【衍】 appear *v.* 出現；顯得

▶ appliance [ə'plaɪəns]

【釋】 *n.* 電器用具

【例】 Change the floors and add new cupboards or *appliances*.

▶ appreciate [ə'priʃɪet]

【釋】 *v.* 欣賞

【例】 You won't be able to *appreciate* the artwork or get a good look at anything with so much going on, with so many people moving around.

【衍】 appreciation *n.* 欣賞

【近】 enjoy

▶ approach [əˈprotʃ]

【釋】 *n.* 方法

【例】 One *approach*, or strategy, sets the initial price of the product high followed by a lower price at a later stage.

【衍】 approachable *adj.* 親近的

【近】 method, way

▶ appropriate [əˈproprɪət]

【釋】 *adj.* 合適的

【例】 Well, I don't think it's *appropriate* to use class time for that kind of thing.

【衍】 appropriately *adv.* 適當地

【近】 suitable, proper

▶ aptly [ˈæptlI]

【釋】 *adv.* 適當地

【例】 The *aptly* named water-hold-ing frog, for example, has a bladder that is highly elastic and stretchable.

【衍】 apt *adj.* 恰當的

【近】 properly

▶ aqueduct [ˈækwɪˌdʌkt]

【釋】 *n.* 渡槽

【例】 They built structures called *aqueducts*.

【衍】 aqueous *adj.* 水的

【近】 conduit

▶ archaeologist [ˌɑrkɪˈɑlədʒɪst]

【釋】 *n.* 考古學家

【例】 For example, in the deserts of Egypt, *archaeologists* have found tombs more than two thousand years old.

【衍】 archaeology *n.* 考古學

▶ architecture [ˈɑrkəˌtɛktʃɚ]

【釋】 *n.* 建築風格

【例】 But, I really fell in love with the *architecture* of the house, the unusual way it was designed and built, so I convinced my wife that we could hire people to fix it up and make the house nice.

【衍】 architectural *adj.* 建築學的

▶ arid [ˈærɪd]

【釋】 *adj.* 乾旱的

【例】 And artifacts don't decay as fast in *arid* climates.

【衍】 aridity *n.* 乾旱；乏味

▶ arithmetic [əˈrɪθmətɪk]

【釋】 *n.* 算術

【例】 They say there's evidence that babies as young as five months old can do basic *arithmetic*—they can add.

【衍】 arithmetical *adj.* 算術的

【近】 algorithm

▶ arouse [əˈrauz]

【釋】 *v.* 喚起

【例】 Artists use these visual effects and the senses they *arouse* to give meaning to their work.

【衍】 arousing *adj.* 振奮人心的

【近】 cause

▶ artifact [ˈɑrtɪˌfækt]

【釋】 *n.* 文物

【例】 But why are some *artifacts* preserved well enough to last for thousands of years?

【衍】 artifactitious *adj.* 人工製品的

【近】 artefact

▶ aside [ə'saɪd]

【釋】 *adv.* 在旁邊

【例】 Someone was working away at a point, then had to stop, and put it *aside* in one of these caches to work on later.

【近】 alongside

▶ assemble [ə'sɛmbl]

【釋】 *v.* 集合

【例】 What they did was they *assembled* a group of subjects, a group of students, and they showed these students a series of geometrical shapes.

【衍】 assembling *adj.* 裝配的；組合的 *n.* 裝配

【近】 aggregate

▶ assistant [ə'sɪstənt]

【釋】 *n.* 助手

【例】 I worked as a research *assistant* in a laboratory.

【衍】 assistance *n.* 援助 assist *v.* 幫助 *n.* 幫助

【近】 helper

▶ assortment [ə'sɔrtmənt]

【釋】 *n.* 種類

【例】 Instead, students will be offered a wide *assortment* of cold breakfast items in the morning.

【衍】 assort *v.* 協調；把……抽成一類 assorted *adj.* 各式各樣的

【近】 classification, category

▶ **assume** [ə'sum]

【釋】 *v.* 假設

【例】 So, when we look at lakes, they seem to be permanent. We *assume* they'll be around forever.

【衍】 assumed *adj.* 假定的 assumption *n.* 設想 assuming *adj.* 傲慢的

【近】 presume

▶ **attempt** [ə'tɛmpt]

【釋】 *v.* 試圖

【例】 Individual members of a group *attempt* to conform their opinions to what they believe to be the group consensus even though the result may be negative.

【衍】 attempted *adj.* 企圖的

【近】 undertake

▶ **attribute** ['ætrəˌbjut]

【釋】 *v.* 把……歸於

【例】 Having little understanding of natural causes, it *attributes* both desirable and undesirable occurrences to supernatural or magical forces, and it searches for means to win the favor of these forces.

【衍】 attributive *adj.* 定語的；歸屬的 attribution *n.* 歸因；屬性

▶ **audit** ['ɔdɪt]

【釋】 *v.* 稽核

【例】 Many universities allow students to *audit* classes.

【衍】 auditorial *adj.* 查帳的

▶ auditorium [ˌɔdɪ'tɔrɪəm]

【釋】 *n.* 禮堂

【例】 They're gonna be performing in the *auditorium* next Saturday.

【衍】 auditory *adj.* 聽覺的

▶ automatically [ˌɔtə'mætɪklɪ]

【釋】 *adv.* 自動地

【例】 These procedural memories allow people to perform the action *automatically* and to recall it relatively easily many years later.

【衍】 automatic *adj.* 自動的 automate *v.* 使自動化

【近】 voluntarily

▶ bacteria [bæk'tɪrɪə]

【釋】 *n.* 細菌（複數）

【例】 *Bacteria*, like all living things, depend on oxygen to grow.

【衍】 bacterial *adj.* 細菌的 bacterium *n.* 細菌（單數）

【近】 microbe

▶ bake [bek]

【釋】 *v.* 烘焙

【例】 Margarine is butter's substitute and you can *bake* equally well with either.

【衍】 bakery *n.* 麵包店 baker *n.* 麵包師

▶ barely ['bɛrlɪ]

【釋】 *adv.* 幾乎不

【例】 Yeah, I *barely* even knew how to do those things when I first came here.

【衍】 bare *adj.* 空的；赤裸的 *v.* 露出

【近】 hardly

▶ **barrier** ['bærɪɚ]

【釋】 *n.* 屏障

【例】 The covering acts like a *barrier* that locks in moisture.

【近】 block

▶ **base** [bes]

【釋】 *n.* 基礎

【例】 For example, a company that sells skis might have a large customer *base* that enjoys winter sports like skiing down snowy mountains.

【衍】 basis *n.* 基礎的 basic *adj.* 基礎的

【近】 basis

▶ **beak** [bik]

【釋】 *n.* 鳥嘴

【例】 A hummingbird comes around and sticks its *beak* into the flowers to get the nectar out.

【衍】 beaked *adj.* 有喙的 beakless *adj.* 無喙的

▶ **bean** [bin]

【釋】 *n.* 豆

【例】 Say, *bean* plants.

▶ **beetle** ['bitl]

【釋】 *n.* 甲殼蟲

【例】 For example, some trees in the forest are poisonous to *beetles*.

▶ behavior [bɪˈhevjɚ]

【釋】 *n.* 行為

【例】 Our thinking and *behavior* are often influenced by other people.

【衍】 behave *v.* 表現 behavioral *adj.* 行為的

▶ belief [bɪˈlif]

【釋】 *n.* 信仰

【例】 Cultures tend to resist ideas that seem to foreign, too different from their own *beliefs* and values.

【衍】 believe 相信

【近】 faith

▶ beneath [bɪˈniθ]

【釋】 *prep.* 在……之下

【例】 For example, in the Sahara Desert, in Africa, there's a type of lizard that's able to move *beneath* the surface, through the sand, very quickly.

【近】 under

▶ benefit [ˈbɛnɪfɪt]

【釋】 *v.* 受益於

【例】 Some animals, though, actually *benefit* from forest fires.

【衍】 beneficial *adj.* 有益的

【近】 profit

▶ beverage [ˈbɛvərɪdʒ]

【釋】 *n.* 飲料

【例】 Also, if food were allowed in classroom, it would be possible for us to have in-class parties on the last day of class—with snack foods and *beverages*—to celebrate the end of each semester.

【近】 drink

▶ bias ['baɪəs]

【釋】 *n.* 偏差

【例】 This tendency is often referred to as the comfort zone *bias*.

【衍】 biased *adj.* 有偏見的

▶ bill [bɪl]

【釋】 *n.* 帳單

【例】 I don't want to get stuck with having to pay for most of the *bill*.

【衍】 billing *n.* 廣告；記帳；開發票

▶ biotic [baɪ'ɑtɪk]

【釋】 *adj.* 生物的

【例】 The number of humans, animals, insects, or plants living in a given area can vary because of two kinds of factors：*biotic* and abiotic.

【衍】 biotechnology *n.* 生物技術

【近】 biological

▶ bite [baɪt]

【釋】 *v.* 咬

【例】 A long long time ago, a dog sensing danger would get ready to *bite* whatever animal that was threatening it.

【衍】 biting *adj.* 刺痛的

▶ bladder ['blædɚ]

【釋】 *n.* 膀胱

【例】 When it does rain, the frog absorbs water through its skin and its *bladder* stretches to hold this extra water.

▶ blend [blɛnd]

【釋】 *v.* 融合

【例】 This camouflage helps to disguise them from predators by enabling them to *blend* into, uh, a specific part of the sea.

【衍】 blended *adj.* 混雜的

【近】 compound

▶ board [bɔrd]

【釋】 *n.* 木板

【例】 An important additional feature of the lounge will be a bulletin *board* on the wall for posting and sharing information that may be especially useful to commuter students and their particular needs.

【衍】 boarding *adj.* 供膳的 *n.* 上船；木板

▶ booklet ['buklɪt]

【釋】 *n.* 小冊子

【例】 And I'm sure that *booklet* was mailed to lots of other people who also rent.

【近】 pamphlet

▶ boring ['bɔrɪŋ]

【釋】 *adj.* 無聊的

【例】 I myself have taken these three-hour seminars and

034 | 單字表 1

found them tiring and sometimes *boring*.

【衍】 bore *v.* 使無聊 bored *adj.* 感到無聊的

 bowl [bol]

【釋】 *n.* 碗

【例】 It got its name because of the formation of its leaves creates a kind of urn or *bowl* where it can store water.

【衍】 bowling *n.* 保齡球

▶ **branch** [bræntʃ]

【釋】 *n.* 樹枝

【例】 So, for instance, let's say a large number of ants are walking on a tree toward some food on a *branch*.

【衍】 branching *adj.* 分支的
branchless *adj.* 無枝的

▶ **bread** [brɛd]

【釋】 *n.* 麵包

【例】 So, for example, say a man who baked *bread* wanted a new coat.

▶ **bridge** [brɪdʒ]

【釋】 *n.* 橋梁

【例】 Then, one after another, other ants do the same thing until enough ants connect together to form a *bridge* between the two branches.

▶ **briefcase** ['brifkes]

【釋】 *n.* 公文包

【例】 So back to our biology lecture, you start talking about frogs and then you pull a live frog out of your *brief-case*.

【近】 portfolio

▶ **briefly** [ˈbriflɪ]

【釋】 *adv.* 簡要地

【例】 *Briefly* summarize the problem, then state which solution you recommend and explain why.

【衍】 brief *adj.* 簡短的

▶ **broadcast** [ˈbrɔdkæst]

【釋】 *v.* 播放

【例】 She needs people to watch various new TV programs that haven't been *broadcast* yet.

【衍】 broadcaster *n.* 廣播公司；廣播員

▶ **brochure** [broˈʃur]

【釋】 *n.* 小冊子

【例】 They made little books with information about the macaw, with pictures, full colored pictures of the macaw that showed off its beautiful feathers, and they passed out these little books, these informational *brochures*.

▶ **budget** [ˈbʌdʒɪt]

【釋】 *n.* 預算

【例】 So I don't think it's going to put any strain on the university's *budget*.

【衍】 budgetary *adj.* 預算的

▶ **bulletin** ['bulətən]

【釋】 *n.* 公告

【例】 He added that posters can instead be displayed in the dining hall. Students can use the *bulletin* board in the dining hall for posters, so the policy change should not be a problem.

【近】 announcement

▶ **bump** [bʌmp]

【釋】 *v.* 碰

【例】 Tina, I'm so glad I *bump* into you.

【衍】 bumpy *adj.* 顛簸的

單字表 2

▶ burst [bɝst]

【釋】 *v.* 爆裂

【例】 I think some of the pipes *burst* or wore out or something.

▶ bushy [buʃɪ]

【釋】 *adj.* 濃密的

【例】 They have a big white stripe that runs from the top of their head all the way down their back and along their big *bushy* tail.

【衍】 bush *n.* 灌木

▶ butter ['bʌtɚ]

【釋】 *n.* 奶油

【例】 So, uh, you see, increase of the price of *butter* increases the demand for margarine.

▶ butterfly ['bʌtɚflaɪ]

【釋】 *n.* 蝴蝶

【例】 And parts of the morpho *butterfly* wings are very shiny.

▶ cafeteria [ˌkæfə'tɪrɪə]

【釋】 *n.* 自助餐廳

【例】 And if they include the *cafeteria* menu for the day in the email, then people are definitely gonna read it.

▶ cage [kedʒ]

【釋】 *n.* 籠子

【例】 The leaf quickly closes to form a little *cage*, trapping the insect between the leaves.

▶ camouflage [ˈkæməˌflɑʒ]

【釋】 *n.* 偽裝

【例】 But when it enters other environments without these green plants, its *camouflage* doesn't work any more.

▶ campus [ˈkæmpəs]

【釋】 *n.* 大學

【例】 The administration has announced plans to acquire a new sculpture for *campus*.

▶ capable [ˈkepəbl]

【釋】 *adj.* 能幹的

【例】 Let's talk about an experiment that may show that babies could be *capable* of feeling empathy.

【衍】 capability *n.* 才能

【近】 competent

▶ capture [ˈkæptʃɚ]

【釋】 *v.* 捕捉

【例】 Carnivorous plants *capture* insects in different ways.

【衍】 capturer *n.* 捕獲者

▶ cardboard [ˈkɑrdbɔrd]

【釋】 *n.* 硬紙板

【例】 Instead of selling their cookies in a plain *cardboard* box, they might sell them in a nice metal box.

【近】 hardboard

▶ carnivorous [kɑrˈnɪvərəs]

【釋】 *adj.* 食肉的

【例】 They are called *carnivorous* plants.

【衍】 carnivore *n.* 食肉動物

▶ cave [kev]

【釋】 *n.* 洞穴

【例】 Millions of them live to-gether in the same *cave*.

【衍】 cavernous *adj.* 空洞的

【近】 hole

▶ cement [sə'mɛnt]

【釋】 *n.* 水泥

【例】 I think these trails should be paved with *cement*.

▶ centimeter ['sɛntə,mitɚ]

【釋】 *n.* 公分

【例】 It's only about 18 or 20 *centimeters* tall.

▶ cereal ['sɪrɪəl]

【釋】 *n.* 麥片

【例】 Sure it is! But are they saying yogurt is better for you than an omelet or than hot *cereal*? I mean, whether something is hot or cold, that shouldn't be the issue.

▶ ceremony ['sɛrə,monɪ]

【釋】 *n.* 儀式

【例】 Traditionally, the university holds one *ceremony* for all graduating students, during which students are awarded their diplomas.

【衍】 ceremonial *adj.* 儀式的

▶ channel ['tʃænl]

【釋】 *n.* 水管渠道

【例】 Now, aqueducts are series of open *channels*, waterways that stretch from water sources high in the mountains to cities.

▶ chaotic [ke'ɑtɪk]

【釋】 *adj.* 混亂的

【例】 Well, these elements together can convey a wilder, more *chaotic* emotion in the viewer, more than say a painting with tiny, smooth brush strokes and soft or pale colors.

【衍】 chaos *n.* 混亂

▶ chapter ['tʃæptɚ]

【釋】 *n.* 章節

【例】 Well, since we only have to read a couple of *chapters*

at a time, you're welcome to share my copy for a few weeks.

▶ chase [tʃes]

【釋】 *v.* 追逐

【例】 Tens of thousands of years ago, though, the lions were there *chasing* the pronghorns.

▶ chemistry ['kɛmɪstrɪ]

【釋】 *n.* 化學

【例】 The bus I was taking is leaving earlier now and I can't get to it in time because I've got *chemistry* class then.

【衍】 chemical *adj.* 化學的

▶ choir ['kwaɪɚ]

【釋】 *n.* 唱詩班

【例】 Well, you know I'm in the *choir*, right? And we have a concert in an hour, just an hour from now.

▶ cite [saɪt]

【釋】 *v.* 列舉

【例】 Administrators *cite* two reasons for the change.

【衍】 citation *n.* 引用

▶ civilization [ˌsɪvlə'zeʃən]

【釋】 *n.* 文明

【例】 And they examine these artifacts to learn about past *civilizations*.

【衍】 civilized *adj.* 文明的

▶ claw [klɔ]

【釋】 *n.* 爪子

【例】 For example, the mole, a small, furry mammal, has really wide, super strong front feet with big *claws*.

▶ climb [klaɪm]

【釋】 *v.* 爬

【例】 Many mountain animals have strong muscles that help them *climb* up and down the steep slopes.

▶ clutter ['klʌtɚ]

【釋】 *v.* 混亂

【例】 Dodger's picture looks more *cluttered*, more crowded with details than the pictures of other artists, because its entire surface is painted and there are no spaces left empty.

▶ cognitive ['kɑgnətɪv]

【釋】 *adj.* 認知的

【例】 These contradictions can cause a kind of mental discomfort known as *cognitive* dissonance.

【衍】 cognition *n.* 認識 cognize *v.* 認知

▶ colony ['kɑlənɪ]

【釋】 *n.* 殖民地

【例】 Some members of the colony are responsible for providing appropriate food for the entire *colony*.

【衍】 colonial *adj.* 殖民的 colonist *n.* 殖民者

▶ coloration [ˌkʌlə'reʃən]

【釋】 *n.* 保護色

【例】 Many animals use *coloration* to protect themselves from predators.

▶ combine [kəm'baɪn]

【釋】 *v.* 結合

【例】 Artists *combine* and manipulate these visual elements to express a message or to create a mood.

【衍】 combined *adj.* 組合的

▶ commitment [kə'mɪtmənt]

【釋】 *n.* 承諾

【例】 This is known as irrational *commitment*.

【衍】 committed *adj.* 堅定的 commit *v.* 犯罪;把……託付給

▶ commute [kə'mjut]

【釋】 *n.* 通勤

【例】 Oh, so you have a pretty long *commute* to campus then? Yeah.

【衍】 commuter *n.* 通勤者

▶ compact ['kɑmpækt]

【釋】 *adj.* 結實的

【例】 In other words, their bodies are often more *compact* than other animals'.

【衍】 compactly *adv.* 簡潔地

▶ compare [kəm'pɛr]

【釋】 *v.* 比較

【例】 We *compare* the two reports carefully.

【衍】 comparative *adj.* 比較的

▶ compete [kəm'pit]

【釋】 *v.* 競爭

【例】 There won't be any weeds to *compete* with them for crucial resources.

【衍】 competitive *adj.* 競爭的 competition *n.* 比賽

▶ complexity [kəm'plɛksɪtɪ]

【釋】 *n.* 複雜性

【例】 The behavior of the insects as a group demonstrates a greater level of *complexity* than the behavior of individual group members.

【衍】 complex *adj.* 複雜的

【近】 sophistication

▶ component [kəm'ponənt]

【釋】 *n.* 組成部分

【例】 It's really the visual *components* of the work, things like color, texture, shape, lines and how these elements work together that tell us something about the work.

▶ concentrate ['kɑnsn͵tret]

【釋】 *v.* 專注

【例】 So, I guess I could just *concentrate* on getting the other two papers done first.

【衍】 concentration *n.* 注 意 力 concentrated *adj.* 集中的

【近】 focus

▶ concentration [͵kɑnsn'treʃən]

【釋】 *n.* 注意力

【例】 Yeah! It will interfere with everyone's *concentration*.

【衍】 concentrate *v.* 專注 concentrated *adj.* 集中的

▶ conceptual [kən'sɛptʃuəl]

【釋】 *adj.* 概念上的

【例】 Photography also affected painting in a more *conceptual* way.

【衍】 concept *n.* 概念

▶ concert ['kɑnsɚt]

【釋】 *n.* 音樂會

【例】 And sometimes some of us would get together on the weekend, maybe for a *concert* or a baseball game or something.

▶ concessively [kən'sesɪvlɪ]

【釋】 *adv.* 讓步地

【例】 (*Concessively*) Yeah, you do get to participate more.

【衍】 concessive *adj.* 讓步的

▶ concrete ['kɑŋkrit]

【釋】 *n.* 混凝土

【例】 Because of this special *concrete,* they could build better bridges, bridges that could go across wide rivers, bridges that were big enough to transport equipment and materials with wagons and carts.

【衍】 concretely *adv.* 具體地

▶ condiment ['kɑndɪmənt]

【釋】 *n.* 調味品

【例】 Companies started using plastic containers for *condiments* such as ketchup, mustard and mayonnaise.

▶ cone [kon]

【釋】 *n.* 圓錐形

【例】 The leaves are slightly overlapping and are tightly rolled into a kind of *cone* shape or a funnel shape.

【近】 conoid

▶ conflict ['kɑnflɪkt]

【釋】 *n.* 衝突

【例】 I eliminated the *conflict,* at least in my mind.

【衍】 conflicting *adj.* 衝突的

【近】 interference

▶ congregate ['kɑŋgrɪget]

【釋】 *v.* 聚集

【例】 So instead of spreading all

over the country side, the workers started to *congregate* in the village with the factory.

【衍】 congregation *n.* 集合；集會

▶ conjure ['kʌndʒɚ]

【釋】 *v.* 令人想起

【例】 The color red, for example, is a strong color, and can *conjure* up strong emotions such as extreme joy or excitement or even anger.

【衍】 conjurer *n.* 巫師 conjuration *n.* 魔法

▶ conquest ['kɑŋkwɛst]

【釋】 *n.* 征服

【例】 Now diffusion can occur through a variety of ways：military *conquest* or tourism or even something like the influence of satellite TV shows around the world.

【衍】 conqueror *n.* 征服者 conquer *v.* 征服

【近】 defeat

▶ conscious ['kɑnʃəs]

【釋】 *adj.* 意識到的

【例】 When they're *conscious* of being observed, they'll likely begin typing at a much faster rate than they would if they were alone.

【衍】 consciousness *n.* 意識；知覺

【近】 aware

▶ consequence ['kɑnsəkwɛns]

【釋】 n. 後果

【例】 An unpleasant *consequence*, on the other hand, discourages further repetition of the behavior.

【衍】 consequent *adj.* 隨之發生的 consequential *adj.* 結果的；重要的

【近】 outcome

▶ consider [kən'sɪdɚ]

【釋】 v. 思考

【例】 All right, so let's *consider* the works of outsider artist Henry Dodger.

【衍】 considerable *adj.* 相當大的；重要的 considerate *adj.* 體貼的；考慮周到的

▶ consist [kən'sɪst]

【釋】 v. 組成

【例】 The classroom component *consists* of seminars on that country's culture, politics, and economy.

【衍】 consistent *adj.* 一致的 consistency *n.* 一致性

【近】 make up, be composed of

▶ consistency [kən'sɪstənsɪ]

【釋】 n. 一致性

【例】 Think of it as a *consistency*.

【衍】 consistent *adj.* 一致的 consist *v.* 組成

【近】 conformance

▶ constancy ['kɑnstənsɪ]

【釋】 n. 穩定性

【例】 This is what is known as

perceptual *constancy*.

【衍】 constant *adj.* 不變的

▶ consumer [kən'sumɚ]

【釋】 *n.* 消費者

【例】 If a *consumer* has to choose between two products, what determines the choice? Assume that someone, a purchaser, is choosing between two products that cost the same.

【近】 customer

▶ container [kən'tenɚ]

【釋】 *n.* 容器

【例】 So the design of the *container* is very important.

【衍】 contain *v.* 包含

▶ context ['kantɛkst]

【釋】 *n.* 環境

【例】 If not for perceptual constancy, we might have difficulty recognizing familiar objects if we viewed them in a new and different *context*.

【衍】 contextual *adj.* 上下文的

【近】 circumstance

▶ continual [kən'tɪnjuəl]

【釋】 *adj.* 不斷的

【例】 Biotic and abiotic factors cause *continual* changes in the number of individuals that make up a population of organisms.

【衍】 continue *v.* 繼續 continued *adj.* 持久的

【近】 frequent

▶ continuous [kən'tɪnjuəs]

【釋】 *adj.* 連續的

【例】 However, if through *continuous* and prolonged exposure the animal learns that the situation is harmless the behavior gradually diminishes.

【衍】 continue *v.* 繼續 continued *adj.* 持久的

▶ contorted [kən'tɔrtɪd]

【釋】 *adj.* 扭曲的

【例】 Meanwhile, I was shaking my hand as if that would stop my thumb from hurting and my face was *contorted* in pain.

【衍】 contort *v.* 扭曲

▶ contradict [ˌkɑntrə'dɪkt]

【釋】 *v.* 矛盾

【例】 Under the circumstances that nonverbal languages and verbal languages *contradict* in the contents they express, nonverbal languages are more likely to release people's true emotions.

【衍】 contradiction *n.* 矛盾 contradictory *adj.* 矛盾的

▶ contradiction [ˌkɑntrə'dɪkʃən]

【釋】 *n.* 矛盾

【例】 Individuals sometimes experience a *contradiction* between their actions and their beliefs—between what they are doing and what they believe they should be doing.

【衍】 contradict *v.* 矛 盾 contra-dictory *adj.* 矛盾的

▶ contrast ['kɑntræst]

【釋】 *n.* 對比

【例】 Remember, you need a balance of unity and *contrast*.

【衍】 contrastive *adj.* 對比的

▶ contribute [kən'trɪbjut]

【釋】 *v.* 捐獻

【例】 I've tried to get in touch with the club members but only four have gotten back to me and said they could *contribute* some money for the cause.

【衍】 contributive *adj.* 有貢獻的 contribution *n.* 貢獻

▶ convince [kən'vɪns]

【釋】 *v.* 說服

【例】 Yeah, but, maybe if other students have the same problem you might be able to *convince* him.

【衍】 convinced *adj.* 確信的 convincing *adj.* 令人信服的

▶ cookware ['kukwɛr]

【釋】 *n.* 炊具

【例】 And she also said that she realized that when people went shopping for new *cookware*, they might feel that they just didn't want to spend all that money on such expensive pots and pans since there were so many in the store that cost a lot less.

【衍】 cooker *n.* 炊具

▶ council ['kaunsl]

【釋】 *n.* 委員會

【例】 The student *council* doesn't even have a vice president.

【衍】 counselor *n.* 顧問

【近】 committee

▶ counteract [ˌkaʊntə'ækt]

【釋】 *v.* 抵制

【例】 In an effort to *counteract* the trend, the college has announced a plan to renovate its on-campus housing.

【衍】 counteractive *adj.* 反作用的
counteraction *n.* 中和；抵抗

▶ co-worker ['ko͵wɝkɝ]

【釋】 *n.* 同事

【例】 So, one day a *co-worker* and I suggested we should give our computers a design makeover: make them look more up-to-date.

【近】 colleague

▶ crack [kræk]

【釋 1】 *n.* 裂縫

【例】 It rains and water gets into the *crack* and stays there.

【衍】 cracker *n.* 餅乾；爆竹
cracked *adj.* 破裂的

【釋 2】 *v.* 破裂；開啟

【例】 The bird has to *crack* open its hard shell.

【近】 fracture, crevasse

▶ creature ['kritʃɚ]

【釋】 *n.* 生物；動物

【例】 Now, as you know, a snail is a very small *creature*.

【近】 animal

▶ creep [krip]

【釋】 *n.* 蔓延

【例】 This phenomenon is known as scope *creep*, and it can cause conflict between businesses and their clients.

【衍】 creeping *adj.* 爬 行 的； 遲緩的

▶ crevasse [krə'væs]

【釋】 *n.* 裂縫

【例】 As the tree grows over the years, the tree's roots extend downward into the crack and *crevasses* of the rock in search of water and nutrients.

【近】 crack, fracture

▶ crinkle ['krɪŋkl]

【釋】 *v.* 使……變皺

【例】 Well, like the part about how it'll help students concentrate, I mean, maybe a little snack will help the person who's eating it, but, the trouble is that it makes it hard for everyone else to concentrate cause they have to listen to someone munching on chips, or biting into an apple, or *crinkling* paper wrappers.

【衍】 crinkled *adj.* 皺的

【近】 wrinkle

▶ critical ['krɪtɪkl]

【釋】 *adj.* 批評的

【例】 There are people who are *critical* of advertising.

【衍】 criticize *v.* 批評 critic *n.* 批評家；評論家

▶ cross [krɔs]

【釋】 *v.* 穿過

【例】 Now, none of these ants alone can *cross* this wide space to get to the other branch with the food.

▶ crow [kro]

【釋】 *n.* 烏鴉

【例】 There's a bird, a species of *crow*, that lives near the water.

▶ crucial ['kruʃəl]

【釋】 *adj.* 主要的

【例】 There won't be any weeds to compete with them for *crucial* resources.

【衍】 crucially *adv.* 主要地

【近】 important

▶ culinary ['kʌlɪnɛrɪ]

【釋】 *adj.* 烹飪的

【例】 During the last week of each semester, the dining hall will feature special meals prepared by the university's *culinary* arts students.

【近】 cooking

▶ cultural ['kʌltʃərəl]

【釋】 *adj.* 文化的

【例】 Now let's talk about a particular *cultural* process: diffusion.

【衍】 culture *n.* 文化

▶ cupboard ['kʌbɚd]

【釋】 *n.* 櫥櫃

【例】 Change the floors, and add new *cupboards* or appliances.

▶ cushion ['kuʃən]

【釋】 *n.* 靠墊

【例】 Uh, let's see, you could throw bright red *cushions* on your dark green sofa for example.

【衍】 cushioning *n.* 緩衝器；軟墊

▶ debris [də'bri]

【釋】 *n.* 碎片

【例】 This is because insects, dead leaves from other plants or other *debris* land on the leaves and then get washed down into the stored water.

▶ decay [dɪ'ke]

【釋1】 *v.* 腐爛

【例】 Artifacts don't *decay* as fast in arid climates.

【衍】 decayed *adj.* 腐爛的

【釋2】 *n.* 腐爛

【例】 They can't grow and cause *decay*.

▶ decompose [ˌdikəm'poz]

【釋】 *v.* 分解

【例】 Gradually they *decompose*.

【衍】 decomposition *n.* 分 解；腐爛；變質 decomposable *adj.* 可分解的

▶ decoration [͵dɛkəˈreʃən]

【釋】 *n.* 裝飾

【例】 So we're talking about interior design, uh, specifically the basic principles typically used in home and office *decoration* in the United States.

【衍】 decorate *v.* 裝飾；佈置 decorated *adj.* 裝飾的；修飾的

▶ defect [ˈdɪfɛkt]

【釋】 *n.* 缺陷

【例】 So product reliability means, basically, the absence of *defects* or problems that you weren't expecting.

【衍】 defective *adj.* 有缺陷的 defector *n.* 背叛者；逃兵

【近】 vice, disadvantage

單字表 3

▶ deliberate [dɪ'lɪbərət]

【釋】 *adj.* 刻意的

【例】 While it is not a *deliberate* behavior, the consequence of social loafing is less personal efficiency when working in groups than when working on one's own.

【近】 intended

▶ delicate ['dɛləkət]

【釋】 *adj.* 微妙的

【例】 Effective designs create a *delicate* balance between two things: you need unity and you also need contrast, which is essentially a break in unity.

【衍】 delicately *adv.* 精緻地；微妙地

▶ demonstrate ['dɛmən͵stret]

【釋】 *v.* 展示

【例】 Now, another strategy is to *demonstrate* something about the product.

【衍】 demonstrative *adj.* 說明的；證明的 demonstration *n.* 示範

【近】 prove

▶ dense [dɛns]

【釋】 *adj.* 密集的

【例】 In rain forests, the canopy produced by the upper layer of branches may be so *dense* that few plants can grow on the shady ground below.

【衍】 densely *adv.* 濃密地 density *n.* 密度

▶ deposit [dɪ'pɑzɪt]

【釋】 *n.* 押金

【例】 Over millions of years, groundwater left *deposits* of a mineral called "calcite" on the rock within Devils Hole.

【衍】 deposition *n.* 沉積物

▶ desert ['dɛzɚt]

【釋】 *n.* 沙漠

【例】 But for frogs who live in dry places, with *desert*— like conditions, this can be a problem.

【衍】 deserted *adj.* 荒蕪的

▶ desire [dɪ'zaɪɚ]

【釋】 *n.* 期望

【例】 Target marketing is the strategy of advertising to smaller, very specific audiences—audiences that have been determined to have the greatest need or *desire* for the product being marketed.

【衍】 desirable *adj.* 令人滿意的

【近】 wish

▶ destructive [dɪ'strʌktɪv]

【釋】 *adj.* 破壞性的

【例】 So by acting out *destructive* behaviors during play, the problem is solved.

【衍】 destruction *n.* 毀滅

【近】 harmful

▶ detection [dɪ'tɛkʃən]

【釋】 *n.* 發覺

【例】 Now many sea animals, in order to hide from predators, have, over time, developed different kinds of camouflage to help them blend in with their environment and avoid *detection* by predators.

【衍】 detective *n.* 偵 探 detect *v.* 察覺；發現

▶ device [dɪ'vaɪs]

【釋】 *n.* 裝置

【例】 University students will be able to download the content of their required textbooks to a reading *device* and read the material directly from the device's screen.

▶ diffusion [dɪ'fjuʒən]

【釋】 *n.* 傳播

【例】 Now let's talk about a particular cultural process: *diffusion*.

【衍】 diffuse *v.* 瀰漫；擴散 *adj.* 瀰漫的

【近】 spread

▶ dig [dɪg]

【釋】 *v.* 挖

【例】 But it doesn't just *dig* a big hole and put all the nuts in it and cover them up.

【衍】 digger *n.* 挖掘機；礦工

▶ digest [daɪ'dʒɛst]

【釋】 *v.* 消化

【例】 The Venus flytrap is then able to *digest* the insect and get its nutrients.

【衍】 digestion *n.* 消化 digestive *adj.* 助消化的

▶ diminish [dɪ'mɪnɪʃ]

【釋】 v. 減弱

【例】 In studies we've found that, when it comes to reproduction, freezing *diminishes* the mating performance of males.

【衍】 diminished *adj.* 減弱的

▶ dioxide [daɪ'ɑksaɪd]

【釋】 n. 二氧化物

【例】 And all the carbon *dioxide* that comes from all those cars on the road is polluting the environment more and more.

▶ diploma [dɪ'plomə]

【釋】 n. 畢業文憑

【例】 Yeah, sure, it takes a long time to have everyone receive their *diploma* individually, especially now that there are more students, but there's an easy way to make it shorter.

▶ disbelief [ˌdɪsbɪ'lif]

【釋】 n. 懷疑

【例】 Suspending *disbelief* enables viewers to become more and more absorbed in the play as they watch the story develop, and to respond emotionally to the events and characters as if they were real.

【衍】 disbelieve *v.* 懷疑

【近】 doubt, suspicion

▶ discomfort [dɪsˈkʌmfɚt]

【釋】 *n.* 不適

【例】 These contradictions can cause a kind of mental *discomfort* known as cognitive dissonance.

▶ discontinue [ˌdɪskənˈtɪnju]

【釋】 *v.* 停止

【例】 The university has decided to *discontinue* its free bus service for students.

【衍】 discontinued *adj.* 停 止 使 用的；不連續的 continue *v.* 繼續

【近】 quit

▶ discover [dɪˈskʌvɚ]

【釋】 *v.* 發現

【例】 I was amazed to *discover* that when I picked it up.

【衍】 discovery *n.* 發現

▶ discuss [dɪˈskʌs]

【釋】 *v.* 討論

【例】 Let's *discuss* some advantages of franchising.

【衍】 discussion *n.* 討論

▶ display [dɪˈsple]

【釋】 *v.* 表現

【例】 However, sometimes an animal species may *display* a behavior that no longer serves a clear purpose.

▶ dispose [dɪˈspoz]

【釋】 *v.* 丟棄

【例】 I think the university should remove these bikes from the racks and *dispose* of them.

【衍】 disposal *n.* 處理；安排 disposable *adj.* 可自由使用的

▶ disregard [ˌdɪsrɪ'gɑrd]

【釋】 *v.* 忽視

【例】 Researchers believe that the primacy effect occurs because after people have made an initial judgment, they tend to notice evidence that supports that judgment, and *disregard* or fail to notice evidence that contradicts it.

【衍】 disregardful *adj.* 不顧的；漠視的

【近】 ignore, neglect

▶ disrupt [dɪs'rʌpt]

【釋】 *v.* 破壞

【例】 If nothing happens to *disrupt* or unbalance the relationship between the animal and its habitat, the carrying capacity will remain stable.

【衍】 disruption *n.* 破壞；分裂 disruptive *adj.* 破壞的；分裂的

【近】 destroy

▶ dissonance ['dɪsənəns]

【釋】 *n.* 失調

【例】 These contradictions can cause a kind of mental discomfort known as cognitive *dissonance*.

【衍】 dissonant *adj.* 刺耳的；不和諧的

【近】 disharmony

▶ distinctive [dɪ'stɪŋktɪv]

【釋】 *adj.* 獨特的

【例】 Skunks have a very *distinctive* marking.

【衍】 distinct *adj.* 明顯的；獨特的 distinction *n.* 區別

【近】 unusual, different

▶ distribute [dɪ'strɪbjut]

【釋】 *v.* 分發

【例】 They *distributed* them to people in schools and community centers in the area.

【衍】 distributed *adj.* 分散的 distribution *n.* 分散；分佈

▶ disturb [dɪ'stɜb]

【釋】 *v.* 打擾

【例】 Yeah, students who are trying to sleep or do works are constantly going to be *disturbed*.

【衍】 disturbance *n.* 打擾；騷亂 disturbing *adj.* 令人不安的

【近】 violate

▶ diverse [daɪ'vɜs]

【釋】 *adj.* 多樣化的

【例】 In this situation, many companies will try to diversify, um, to develop *diverse* product in order to increase sales.

【衍】 diversity *n.* 多樣性；差異 diversify *v.* 使多樣化

【近】 different

▶ document ['dɑkjəmənt]

【釋】 *n.* 文獻

【例】 A big part of the assignment is working with original historical *documents*.

【衍】 documentary *adj.* 記 錄 的
n. 紀錄片

▶ doll [dɑl]

【釋】 *n.* 娃娃

【例】 OK, so the baby looks at the *doll*.

▶ domestication [də͵mɛstə'keʃən]

【釋】 *n.* 馴化

【例】 The *domestication* of animals had a number of benefits for early humans.

【衍】 domestic *adj.* 國內的，家庭的；馴養的

▶ donate ['donet]

【釋】 *v.* 捐贈

【例】 So I don't think we can expect them to *donate* much money for anything else anytime soon.

【衍】 donation *n.* 捐贈

▶ dormitory ['dɔrmətɔrɪ]

【釋】 *n.* 宿舍

【例】 Hmm, well, maybe you should move back into a *dormitory* on campus.

▶ downward ['daunwəd]

【釋】 *adv.* 向下

【例】 Yes, especially unshielded street light, ones that aren't pointed *downward*.

【衍】 down *adv.* 向下 *adj.* 向下的

【近】 alow

▶ dragon ['drægən]

【釋】 *n.* 龍

【例】 A kind of fish like the leafy sea *dragon*, resembles a small green dragon with leaf-like protrusions sticking out like arms.

▶ drastic ['dræstɪk]

【釋】 *adj.* 激烈的

【例】 But still, they're being *drastic*.

【衍】 drastically *adv.* 徹底地；激烈地

【近】 fierce

▶ drastically ['dræstɪkəlɪ]

【釋】 *adv.* 急遽地

【例】 So, when the trees were cut down and cleared away, these animals also didn't have a place to live anymore and their populations *drastically* declined.

【衍】 drastic *adj.* 激烈的

▶ draw [drɔ]

【釋】 *v.* 素描

【例】 The required courses are mostly painting and *drawing*, and they take up all our time.

▶ drawback ['drɔbæk]

【釋】 *n.* 缺點

【例】 In this way, companies can persuade consumers to purchase a product despite its *drawbacks*.

【近】 defect, disadvantage

▶ drop [drɑp]

【釋】 *v.* 下降

【例】 The number would *drop*.

【近】 decline

▶ drought [draut]

【釋】 *n.* 乾旱

【例】 By the time the *drought* ended, the species was extinct.

【衍】 dry *adj.* 乾的

▶ Dutch [dʌtʃ]

【釋】 *adj.* 荷蘭的

【例】 Do you know Rembrandt, the famous *Dutch* painter?

▶ earn [ɜ·n]

【釋】 *v.* 賺取

【例】 Historically, for a very long time, people had made cloth by hand in their homes, *earning* a little money from their home-based cloth production.

【衍】 earner *n.* 賺錢的人

▶ economy [ɪˈkɑnəmɪ]

【釋】 *n.* 經濟

【例】 Let's talk about a couple of the changes that happened as the *economies* of ancient civilizations developed.

【衍】 economic *adj.* 經濟的 economical *adj.* 合算的

▶ editor [ˈɛdɪtɚ]

【釋】 *n.* 編輯

【例】 Do you mean the *editors'* decision?

【衍】 edit *v.* 編 輯 editorial *adj.* 編輯的

▶ effective [ɪ'fɛktɪv]

【釋】 *adj.* 有效的

【例】 Target marketing has proved to be very *effective* in reaching potential customers.

【衍】 effect *n.* 影 響 effectively *adv.* 有效地

▶ efficient [ɪ'fɪʃnt]

【釋】 *adj.* 有效率的

【例】 There are a couple of *efficient* ways that a company can diversify using some of their existing resources.

【衍】 efficiency *n.* 效率

▶ Egypt ['idʒɪpt]

【釋】 *n.* 埃及

【例】 5,000 years ago, *Egypt* really began to flourish out in the Nile River valley.

【衍】 Egyptian *n.* 埃及人 *adj.* 埃及／埃及人的

▶ electricity [ɪ͵lɛk'trɪsətɪ]

【釋】 *n.* 電

【例】 Is there a problem with the *electricity*?

【衍】 electric *adj.* 電的 electrical *adj.* 與電有關的

▶ eliminate [ɪ'lɪmə͵net]

【釋】 *v.* 消除

【例】 This demonstration may help *eliminate* the customer's concerns about buying the computer.

【衍】 elimination *n.* 消除；淘汰

▶ embarrassing [ɪm'bærəsɪŋ]

【釋】 *adj.* 使人尷尬的

【例】 Um, this is a little *embarrassing*.

【衍】 embarrass *v.* 使侷促不安
embarrassed *adj.* 尷尬的

▶ emerge [ɪ'mɝdʒ]

【釋】 *v.* 出現

【例】 As a result, when new technology *emerges*, people may struggle for a time to adapt to it.

【衍】 emerging *adj.* 新興的 emergence *n.* 出現

▶ emit [ɪ'mɪt]

【釋】 *v.* 發射

【例】 So, by *emitting* this chemical, the potato plant protects itself from insects.

【衍】 emitter *n.* 發射器

▶ emotional [ɪ'moʃənl]

【釋】 *adj.* 情緒的

【例】 People with *emotional* intelligence have the ability to recognize their true feelings and understand what is causing them.

【衍】 emotion *n.* 情感 emotionless *adj.* 沒有／不露情感的

▶ empathy ['ɛmpəθi]

【釋】 *n.* 共鳴

【例】 Now, *empathy* is a complex emotion.

【衍】 empathetic *adj.* 同感的

▶ emphasize ['ɛmfəsaɪz]

【釋】 v. 強調

【例】 Now during TV shows that young people watch, shows with pop music or teen serials create a commercial that *emphasizes* how fun the phone is.

【衍】 emphasis *n.* 重點；強調

【近】 stress, highlight

▶ encounter [ɪn'kauntɚ]

【釋】 v. 遭遇

【例】 As we grow older or *encounter* new circumstances, our reference groups may change, and our attitudes and behavior may change accordingly.

【近】 confront

▶ encourage [ɪn'kɚ-rɪdʒ]

【釋】 v. 鼓勵

【例】 Cutting back the bus service and adding parking's just gonna *encourage* more students to drive on campus.

【衍】 encouragement *n.* 鼓勵

▶ endeavor [ɪn'dɛvɚ]

【釋】 *n.* 努力

【例】 This project will provide students with the opportunity to discover the rewards and challenges of working with another individual, an experience that will help them in future *endeavors*.

【近】 effort

▶ engaging [ɪnˈgedʒɪŋ]

【釋】 *adj.* 吸引人的

【例】 In this case, by doing something unexpected, something more *engaging*, you can tap into their passive attention.

【衍】 engage *v.* 吸引；參加
engaged *adj.* 使用中的；忙碌的

【近】 fascinating

▶ enhancement [ɪnˈhænsmənt]

【釋】 *n.* 增強

【例】 It is generally believed that nonverbal languages function as the *enhancement* of emotional expressions when they consist with verbal languages.

【衍】 enhance *v.* 增強；提高

▶ enlarge [ɪnˈlɑrdʒ]

【釋】 *v.* 擴大

【例】 Over time, the roots get bigger and grow deeper, widening and *enlarging* the cracks, causing the rock to break apart.

【衍】 enlargement *n.* 放大

【近】 extend

▶ enormous [ɪˈnɔrməs]

【釋】 *adj.* 巨大的

【例】 Researchers have discovered an *enormous* number of 35,000 year-old thunder bird bones.

【衍】 enormously *adv.* 巨大地

【近】 huge, massive

▶ enrollment [ɪn'rolmənt]

【釋】 *n.* 入學

【例】 Well, the low *enrollment* isn't because art majors don't want to take these classes; the problem is who has time to take them when there are so many other requirements.

【衍】 enroll *v.* 參加；登記

▶ enthusiastic [ɪn͵θuzɪ'æstɪk]

【釋】 *adj.* 熱情的

【例】 Sometimes it means you've been teaching the same subject for 20 years and you're probably tired of it by now and maybe not very *enthusiastic*.

【衍】 enthusiasm *n.* 熱情

【近】 crazy

▶ entrance ['ɛntrəns]

【釋】 *n.* 入口

【例】 I think the lobby at the *entrance* to the student center would be a great location.

【衍】 entranced *adj.* 著迷的

【近】 threshold

▶ essential [ɪ'sɛnʃl]

【釋】 *adj.* 重要的

【例】 The university considers it *essential* that the cost-saving measures not interfere with student activities.

【衍】 essence *n.* 本質；精華 essentially *adv.* 本質上

▶ evaluate [ɪ'vælju͵et]

【釋】 *v.* 評價

【例】 Customers are often willing to pay higher prices for high-quality products; however, without specialized knowledge, it can be difficult to *evaluate* whether certain items are highly quality.

【衍】 evaluation *n.* 評價

【近】 value

▶ eventually [ɪ'vɛntʃuəlɪ]

【釋】 *adv.* 最終地

【例】 When this happens again and again, the crack becomes larger and *eventually* pieces of the rock break off.

【衍】 eventual *adj.* 最後的

【近】 finally, ultimately

▶ evoke [ɪ'vok]

【釋】 *v.* 喚起

【例】 An artist chooses certain colors to *evoke* a particular mood and make powerful statements.

▶ exact [ɪg'zækt]

【釋】 *adj.* 確切的

【例】 And you don't even have to have an *exact* title in mind.

【衍】 exactly *adv.* 恰好地

【近】 precise

▶ exceptionally [ɪk'sɛpʃənəlɪ]

【釋】 *adv.* 異常地

【例】 Maybe it's a man who was *exceptionally* tall.

【衍】 exception *n.* 例外；異議
exceptional *adj.* 異常的；例外的

【近】 singularly

▶ exhausted [ɪɡ'zɔstɪd]

【釋】 *adj.* 精疲力竭的

【例】 You must be *exhausted*.

【衍】 exhaust *v.* 排出；耗盡 exhaustion *n.* 枯竭；耗盡；精疲力竭

【近】 frazzled

▶ exhibit [ɪɡ'zɪbɪt]

【釋1】 *v.* 顯示

【例】 Without being fully aware of it, people who *exhibit* this bias tend to focus on and remember only the advantages of the option they selected.

【衍】 exhibition *n.* 展覽；顯示

【釋2】 *n.* 展覽

【例】 Well, you know how I'm president of the anthro-pology club... well... I'm supposed to drive everyone in the club to see a special *exhibit* at the museum tomorrow.

▶ exist [ɪɡ'zɪst]

【釋】 *v.* 存在

【例】 Psychologists believe that the comfort zone bias *exists* not only because we have a natural preference for what we already know, but also because we want to avoid taking risks.

【衍】 existence *n.* 存在 existing *adj.* 目前的；現存的

【近】 occur

▶ expand [ɪk'spænd]

【釋】 *v.* 擴大

【例】 They had very little means to *expand*.

【衍】 expansion *n.* 膨脹；闡述

▶ expanse [ɪk'spæns]

【釋】 *n.* 廣闊的區域

【例】 This is a serious problem for animals that need access to large *expanse* of land to look for food.

【衍】 expansion *n.* 膨脹；闡述

▶ experiment [ɪk'spɛrəmɛnt]

【釋】 *n.* 實驗

【例】 So they devised an *experiment* in which a baby is shown a doll on a table.

【衍】 experimental *adj.* 實驗的；試驗性的

▶ explanation [ˌɛksplə'neʃən]

【釋】 *n.* 解釋

【例】 One *explanation* is that we remember something better if we already have some previous knowledge about it, some previous understanding of it.

【衍】 explain *v.* 說明；解釋

▶ explicit [ɪk'splɪsɪt]

【釋】 *adj.* 明晰的

【例】 An *explicit* memory is a conscious or intentional recollection, usually of facts, names, events, or other things that a person can state or declare.

【衍】 explicitly *adv.* 明確地；明白地

【近】 precise

▶ **exposure** [ɪk'spoʒɚ]

【釋】 *n.* 暴露

【例】 One benefit of subsurface locomotion is that it enables animals to minimize their *exposure* to extreme temperatures.

【衍】 expose *v.* 揭露；揭發；顯示

【近】 reveal

▶ **expression** [ɪk'sprɛʃən]

【釋】 *n.* 表達

【例】 Nonverbal language refers to human emotional *expressions* without involving verbal statements.

【衍】 express *v.* 表達

▶ **extension** [ɪk'stɛnʃən]

【釋】 *n.* 延期

【例】 But then he did tell us when he gave us the assignment that he wouldn't grant any *extension*.

【衍】 extend *v.* 延伸；擴大

【近】 delay

▶ **external** [ɪk'stɚnl]

【釋】 *adj.* 外部的

【例】 It's the desire to behave in a certain way in order to obtain some kind of *external* reward.

【衍】 externally *adv.* 外部地

【近】 outer

▶ **extinct** [ɪk'stɪŋkt]

【釋】 *adj.* 滅絕的

【例】 But, now, however, lions are all *extinct* in North America; they're no longer predator of the pronghorn.

【衍】 extinction *n.* 滅絕

▶ extinction [ɪk'stɪŋkʃən]

【釋】 *n.* 滅絕

【例】 Well, scientists generally agree that the *extinction* of various animal or plant species is one very likely effect.

【衍】 extinct *v.* 滅絕

▶ extremely [ɪk'strimlɪ]

【釋】 *adv.* 極其

【例】 Now because its colors and shapes, it blends in *extremely* well with green sea plants.

【衍】 extreme *adj.* 極端的

【近】 badly

▶ extrinsic [ɛk'strɪnsɪk]

【釋】 *adj.* 外在的

【例】 As I said, *extrinsic* motivation is external.

【近】 exterior

單字表 4

▶ fabric ['fæbrɪk]

【釋】 *n.* 織物

【例】 We can felt the wool and make it into *fabric*.

【衍】 fabricate *v.* 製造；偽造

【近】 cloth

▶ facial ['feʃəl]

【釋】 *adj.* 面部的

【例】 *Facial* expressions and body movements are the two mostly attributed types of nonverbal languages.

【衍】 face *n.* 臉；表面

▶ facility [fə'sɪlətɪ]

【釋】 *n.* 設施

【例】 I know, that's the point—people don't go there because the *facilities* are old and the exercise equipment breaks down.

【衍】 facilitate *v.* 促進；幫助

▶ factory ['fæktərɪ]

【釋】 *n.* 工廠

【例】 One change was that the center of production moved from homes to *factories*.

【近】 plant

▶ hall [hɔl]

【釋】 *n.* 大廳

【例】 I never eat in the dining *hall*.

▶ hammer ['hæmɚ]

【釋】 *n.* 錘子

【例】 If you hit it with *hammer*, it'll shatter like glass.

▶ handful ['hænd‚ful]

【釋】 *n.* 少數

【例】 "Given the art department's limited budget," the administrator explained, "it just doesn't make sense to hire a new full-time professor to teach sculpture for only a *handful* of students."

▶ handle ['hændl]

【釋】 *v.* 處理

【例】 You could probably *handle* that for a couple of weeks, right?

【衍】 handled *adj.* 有把手的

▶ handout ['hænd‚aut]

【釋】 *n.* 講義

【例】 They have to prepare extra *handouts* for the class.

▶ harden ['hɑrdn]

【釋】 *v.* 變硬

【例】 The Romans developed a special kind of concrete, a building material that would *harden* under water.

【衍】 hard *adj.* 努力的；硬的；困難的

【近】 stiffen

▶ harsh [hɑrʃ]

【釋】 *adj.* 惡劣的

【例】 Even though it's cold and snow-covered, the Arctic houses many species of animals that manage to survive the *harsh* conditions there.

【衍】 harshly *adv.* 嚴厲地；刺耳地

【近】 severe

▶ **hawk** [hɔk]

【釋】 *n.* 鷹

【例】 One type of bird with eyes positioned in the front of the skull is the *hawk*.

【衍】 hawker *n.* 街頭小販

▶ **health** [hɛlθ]

【釋】 *n.* 健康

【例】 I have more energy after I exercise and I know it's good for my *health*.

【衍】 healthy *adj.* 健康的

【近】 fitness

▶ **hectic** [ˈhɛktɪk]

【釋】 *adj.* 忙碌的

【例】 Students' lives are *hectic*, and mealtimes provide important opportunities to take a break and catch up with friends before moving on to the next class or assignment.

▶ **hemisphere** [ˈhɛməsˌfɪr]

【釋】 *n.* 半球

【例】 Pronghorns are, in fact, noted for being the fastest animal in the western *hemisphere*.

【衍】 hemispheric *adj.* 半球的

▶ **herd** [hɝd]

【釋】 *n.* 畜群

【例】 They were easily controlled and organized into *herds* led by shepherd.

【衍】 herder *n.* 牧人

【近】 drove

▶ **high-quality** [ˌhaɪˈkwɑlətɪ]

【釋】 *adj.* 高品質的

【例】 Such a museum would give our students an opportunity to learn to appreciate *high-quality* fine art.

▶ **hike** [haɪk]

【釋】 *n.* 遠足

【例】 In the past, as part of orientation, new, incoming students could go on a two-day *hiking* and camping trip together with other incoming students on the weekend before classes begin.

【衍】 hiker *n.* 旅行者

▶ **historical** [hɪˈstɔrɪkl]

【釋】 *adj.* 歷史的

【例】 There are plenty of *historical* topics.

【衍】 history *n.* 歷史 historic *adj.* 有歷史意義的

▶ **hoarder** [ˈhɔrdɚ]

【釋】 *n.* 囤積者

【例】 Some types of *hoarders* engage in scatter hoarding.

【衍】 hoard *v.* 貯藏

▶ **honor** [ˈɑnɚ]

【釋】 *n.* 榮幸

【例】 Well, it's a huge *honor* to win and there's an award ceremony they've invited.

【衍】 honored *adj.* 受尊敬的 honourable *adj.* 值得尊敬的

084 | 單字表 4

【近】 glory

▶ horizontal [ˈhɑrəˈzɑntl]

【釋】 *adj.* 水平的

【例】 Suppose you tilt the plate to a different angle, to a *horizontal* position, like you're planning to put food on it, still a perfect circle? No! The circle is now stretched out, flattened into an oval.

【衍】 horizon *n.* 地平線；視野

▶ hunt [hʌnt]

【釋】 *v.* 捕殺

【例】 There are these foxes called kit foxes that live in the southwestern United States. They *hunt* small animals like mice and squirrels which are spread out over large areas of open grasslands.

【衍】 hunter *n.* 獵人

▶ hypothesis [haɪˈpɑθəsɪs]

【釋】 *n.* 假設

【例】 Their *hypothesis* is when there was no rainfall, the birds may have flocked together at this lake.

【衍】 hypothetical *adj.* 假設的

【近】 tentative

▶ icy [ˈaɪsɪ]

【釋】 *adj.* 冰的

【例】 Since they spend so much of their time on snowy, *icy* surfaces, whether they are standing on the ground or swimming in the water, they can easily lose heat through their feet.

【衍】 ice *n.* 冰

▶ identification [aɪˌdentɪfɪ'keʃn]

【釋】 *n.* 身分證明

【例】 Second, currently, students who borrow bikes have to leave a cash deposit, which is returned to them when they return the bikes, but I think students should be required to leave their student *identification* cards instead, so they don't have to remember to bring cash.

【衍】 identify *v.* 確定；鑑定；識別

▶ illusion [ɪ'luʒn]

【釋】 *n.* 幻覺

【例】 From his first shows, Loutherbourg showed a knack for imagination and stage design, all in the interest of creating *illusions* that allowed the audience to suspend disbelief completely.

【衍】 illusionary *adj.* 錯覺的；幻影的

【近】 hallucination

▶ illustrate ['ɪləstret]

【釋】 *v.* 說明

【例】 So, this is an example to *illustrate* this.

【衍】 illustration *n.* 說明；插圖；例證

【近】 clarify

▶ illustration [ˌɪləˈstreʃən]

【釋】 *n.* 插圖

【例】 They could look up useful facts and background information on a topic or view different photographs or *illustrations* of something the professor is describing.

【衍】 illustrate *v.* 說明

▶ imitate [ˈɪmɪtet]

【釋】 *v.* 模仿

【例】 By observing the results, or consequences, of another's behavior, people learn, over time, to either *imitate* or avoid imitating that behavior.

【衍】 imitation *n.* 模仿

【近】 simulate

▶ implicit [ɪmˈplɪsɪt]

【釋】 *adj.* 隱形的

【例】 Memories of this kind are called *implicit* memories.

【衍】 implication *n.* 解釋；暗示

▶ impressive [ɪmˈprɛsɪv]

【釋】 *adj.* 令人欽佩的

【例】 And I started working with some really bright, young people who'd already been working in the company for a few years, who were already handling major responsibilities for the company, really *impressive*.

【衍】 impress *v.* 給某人留下印象
impression *n.* 印象

▶ improvement [ɪm'pruvmənt]

【釋】 *n.* 改善

【例】 They have a new manager and I guess she's made some *improvements* in the quality of the food.

【衍】 improve *v.* 改善

▶ inaccurate [ɪn'ækjərət]

【釋】 *adj.* 不準確的

【例】 Sometimes, however, problems occur that lead to *inaccurate* results.

【衍】 inaccuracy *n.* 錯誤

【近】 incorrect

▶ inappropriate [ˌɪnə'proprɪət]

【釋】 *adj.* 不恰當的

【例】 She realized her reaction was *inappropriate*, and she also realized she wasn't really upset with her friend... There was something else bothering her.

【衍】 inappropriately *adv.* 不適當地

【近】 improper

▶ incorporate [ɪn'kɔrpəˌret]

【釋】 *v.* 融入

【例】 Over time, however, their attitudes change, and they successfully *incorporate* the new technology into their daily lives.

【衍】 incorporation *n.* 公司；合併

【近】 merge

▶ indicate ['ɪndəˌket]

【釋】 *v.* 表明

【例】 An individual can have an

experience that he or she cannot consciously recall yet still display reactions that *indicate* the experience has been somehow recorded in his or her brain.

【衍】 indication *n.* 指示；跡象

▶ indirect [ˌɪndəˈrɛkt]

【釋】 *adj.* 間接的

【例】 The evidence is *indirect* because obviously you can't ask a five-month old baby to add up some numbers for you.

【衍】 indirectly *adv.* 間接地 indirection *n.* 間接

▶ individual [ˌɪndəˈvɪdʒuəl]

【釋 1】 *adj.* 個體的

【例】 Such swarms typically include several thousand *individual* insects.

【衍】 individualized *adj.* 有個性的
individualism *n.* 利己主義

【釋 2】 *n.* 個人

【例】 When an *individual* learns through experience that a certain behavior results in pleasant consequences, that behavior is likely to be repeated.

▶ ingredient [ɪnˈgridɪənt]

【釋】 *n.* 成分

【例】 There was an *ingredient* in this soap that was harmful for the environment.

【近】 element

▶ injury ['ɪndʒərɪ]

【釋】 *n.* 傷害

【例】 These animals may make use of another animal species to transport them, without causing any *injury* to the other species.

【衍】 injure *v.* 傷害 injured *adj.* 受傷的

【近】 harm, damage

▶ innovation [,ɪnə'veʃən]

【釋】 *n.* 創新

【例】 Since the beginning of human history, diverse cultures have taken advantage of one another's *innovations* when they've come into contact.

【衍】 innovate *v.* 創新；改變 innovator *n.* 改革者；創新者

▶ insect ['ɪnsɛkt]

【釋】 *n.* 昆蟲

【例】 So an *insect* gets stuck and can't fly away.

▶ insight ['ɪn,saɪt]

【釋】 *n.* 見解

【例】 Furthermore, we feel that current students will offer unique and valuable *insight* into our visitors during these campus tours.

【衍】 insightful *adj.* 有洞察力的

【近】 perception

▶ install [ɪn'stɔl]

【釋】 *v.* 安裝

【例】 They *install* pipes that run from the lake to their farms, and they pump the water out of the lake and into their fields.

【衍】 installation *n.* 安裝；裝置

【近】 fit

▶ instance ['ɪnstəns]

【釋】 *n.* 例項

【例】 So, for *instance*, let's say a large number of ants are walking on a tree toward some food on a branch.

【近】 case

▶ instantaneously [ˌɪnstən'tenɪəslɪ]

【釋】 *adv.* 即刻

【例】 But, uh, they have a lot more mobility because their camouflage allows them to blend in to any environment, and because cuttlefish

have shifting pigments that allow them to change color in a matter of seconds. So they can almost *instantaneously* match their color of their surroundings.

【衍】 instantaneous *adj.* 瞬間的

【近】 swiftly

▶ instead [ɪn'stɛd]

【釋】 *adv.* 相反

【例】 Well, I talked to my boss and she said I could change my work hours and work at night *instead*.

▶ instinctively [ɪn'stɪŋktɪvlɪ]

【釋】 *adv.* 本能地

【例】 When an animal experiences a situation for the first time, particularly one it considers threatening, it may *instinctively* respond by running away or by warning other members of its community with alarm calls.

【衍】 instinctive *adj.* 本能的

▶ institute ['ɪnstɪtut]

【釋】 *n.* 學院

【例】 I won an award from the Creative Writing *Institute* for a story I wrote.

【衍】 institution *n.* 制 度； 公 共機構

【近】 academy

▶ instrument ['ɪnstrəmənt]

【釋】 *n.* 樂器

【例】 Currently, the campus mu-

sic building—which has practice rooms students can reserve for playing *instruments*—closes nightly at nine p.m.

【衍】 instrumental *adj.* 樂器的

▶ insulate ['ɪnsə͵let]

【釋】 *v.* 隔離

【例】 And if they *insulated* the buildings better, these are really old buildings.

【衍】 insulation *n.* 絕緣；孤立

【近】 segregant

▶ integrate ['ɪntə͵gret]

【釋】 *v.* 結合

【例】 While some farmers treat the cultivation of their animals and plants as two separate activities, others *integrate* the two so that they work together.

【衍】 integration *n.* 整合；結合

▶ intellectual [ˌɪntl'ɛktʃuəl]

【釋】 *adj.* 智力的

【例】 Scientists have learned some interesting things about the *intellectual* abilities of babies.

【衍】 intelligent *adj.* 聰明的

▶ intelligent [ɪn'tɛlɪdʒənt]

【釋】 *adj.* 聰明的

【例】 Now, before he started the training, the researcher was told that one group of monkeys was highly *intelligent* and the other group was less intelligent.

【衍】 intellectual *adj.* 智力的 intelligence *n.* 智慧

【近】 wise

▶ intentional [ɪn'tɛnʃənl]

【釋】 *adj.* 有意的

【例】 An explicit memory is a conscious or *intentional* recollection, usually of facts, names, events, or other things that a person can state or declare.

【衍】 intention *n.* 意圖；目的

【近】 designed

▶ interaction [ˌɪntə'rækʃən]

【釋】 *n.* 互動

【例】 This *interaction* is at the heart of social life.

【衍】 interact *v.* 互相影響／作用

▶ interchangeable [ˌɪntəˈtʃendʒəbl]

【釋】 *adj.* 可互換的

【例】 They are similar enough to be *interchangeable*.

【衍】 interchange *v.* 交換

【近】 exchangeable

▶ interfere [ˌɪntəˈfɪr]

【釋】 *v.* 干擾

【例】 Yeah! It will *interfere* with everyone's concentration.

【衍】 interference *n.* 干擾；衝突

▶ interior [ɪnˈtɪrɪə]

【釋】 *adj.* 內部的

【例】 So we're talking about *interior* design, uh, specifically the basic principles typically used in home and office decoration in the United States.

【近】 inner

▶ internal [ɪnˈtɜnl]

【釋】 *adj.* 內部的

【例】 With intrinsic, or *internal* motivation, we want to do something because we enjoy it, or get us a sense of accomplishment from it.

【衍】 internally *adv.* 內部地

【近】 inner

▶ internship [ˈɪntɜnʃɪp]

【釋】 *n.* 實習

【例】 I got a month long *internship* in a town about three hours from here.

【衍】 intern *n.* 實習生

▶ interpret [ɪn'tɜ-prɪt]

【釋】 *v.* 解釋

【例】 And this leaves questions that force the reader to *interpret* the events, to fill in information and decide what the characters' conversation and actions might mean.

【衍】 interpretation *n.* 解釋

【近】 account

▶ intrinsic [ɪn'trɪnsɪk]

【釋】 *adj.* 內在的

【例】 However, *intrinsic* motivation is generally considered to be more long-lasting than the other.

【衍】 intrinsical *adj.* 本質的

【近】 inherent

▶ invalidate [ɪn'vælə‚det]

【釋】 *v.* 使無效

【例】 The researcher expects a particular result from the experiment, and that expectation causes the researcher to act in ways that influence the behavior of the experiment participants, thereby *invalidating* the results of the experiment.

【衍】 invalid *adj.* 無效的

▶ involuntary [ɪn'valən‚tɛrɪ]

【釋】 *adj.* 非自願的

【例】 Now, the other type of attention is passive attention, when it's *involuntary*.

【衍】 involuntarily *adv.* 無心地；不自覺地

▶ involve [ɪn'vɑlv]

【釋】 v. 包括

【例】 Nonverbal language refers to human emotional expressions without *involving* verbal statements.

【衍】 involved *adj.* 有關的 involvement *n.* 參與；牽連

【近】 contain

▶ irrational [ɪ'ræʃənl]

【釋】 *adj.* 非理性的

【例】 This is known as *irrational* commitment.

【衍】 irrationally *adv.* 無理地

【近】 unreasonable

▶ irrelevant [ɪ'rɛləvənt]

【釋】 *adj.* 無關的

【例】 The advertisement is *irrelevant* or useless for them.

【衍】 irrelevance *n.* 離題；不相關的事物

【近】 inconnected

▶ irresponsible [ˌɪrɪ'spɑnsəbl]

【釋】 *adj.* 不負責任的

【例】 I guess if your partner's *irresponsible*, you're out of luck.

【衍】 irresponsibility *n.* 不負責任

▶ isolation [ˌaɪsə'leʃən]

【釋】 *n.* 孤立

【例】 There's just not as much need to work in *isolation*.

【衍】 isolate *v.* 使隔離；*adj.* 孤立的

▶ issue [ˈɪʃu]

【釋】 *n.* (報刊的)期，號，版次

【例】 I don't think we can put together next month's *issue*.

【衍】 issuer *n.* 發行人 issuance *n.* 釋出；發行

【近】 question

▶ jeopardize [ˈdʒɛpɚdaɪz]

【釋】 *v.* 危害

【例】 He thought that disagreeing with them might *jeopardize* his chances of getting a promotion by not looking like a team-player.

【近】 harm

▶ jewelry [ˈdʒuəlrɪ]

【釋】 *n.* 珠寶

【例】 The *jewelry* was worth the high prices.

【衍】 jewel *n.* 珠寶

▶ judgment [ˈdʒʌdʒmənt]

【釋】 *n.* 判斷

【例】 One common signaling strategy is to have a person or company that is not involved in the sale provide an objective, unbiased *judgment* about the quality of a product.

【衍】 judge *v.* 判斷

▶ jut [dʒʌt]

【釋】 *v.* 突出

【例】 Moreover, just look at the sculpture: several 60-foot long steel plates, *jutting* out of the earth at odd angles!

It's just so large that it'll take up all the green space in front of the campus center! This is public space that should be reserved for students to use.

▶ ketchup ['kɛtʃəp]

【釋】 *n.* 番茄醬

【例】 And then you had to either pour the *ketchup* or mustard on your food which could be messy or scoop it out with spoon.

▶ kick [kɪk]

【釋】 *v.* 踢

【例】 He and his friends are always out there on the lawn right where the sculpture will be, *kicking* around the soccer ball.

【衍】 kicking *adj.* 活潑熱烈的

【近】 boot

▶ laboratory ['læbrəˌtɔrɪ]

【釋】 *n.* 實驗室

【例】 Are you still working in Professor Green's *laboratory*?

【近】 lab

▶ lace [les]

【釋】 *n.* 鞋帶

【例】 In one study, college students were asked to each put on a pair of shoes—shoes with *laces* they would have to tie.

【衍】 laced *adj.* 有花邊的

▶ lack [læk]

【釋】 n. 缺失

【例】 "The main reason is a *lack* of student interest," reported one administrator.

【衍】 lacking *adj.* 缺乏的

▶ lamp [læmp]

【釋】 n. 燈

【例】 And there was only just little bit of light from street *lamps*.

▶ lap [læp]

【釋】 n. 膝蓋

【例】 How do you feel about your *lap*?

▶ laptop ['læptɑp]

【釋】 n. 筆記本

【例】 I'll read a book or bring my *laptop* computer and work on a paper for class.

▶ lawn [lɔn]

【釋】 n. 草坪

【例】 *Lawns* may have originated as grassed enclosures within early medieval settlements used for communal grazing of livestock, as distinct from fields reserved for agriculture.

【近】 grass

▶ leadership ['lidɚʃɪp]

【釋】 n. 領導力

【例】 Well, they talked about *leadership* and organizational skills, but that's not really the kind of work you do.

【衍】 lead *n.* 領導 *v.* 引導

▶ leaf [lif]

【釋】 *n.* 樹葉

【例】 The potato plant is able to release a chemical throughout its *leaf* system whenever an insect attacks it, starts eating the leaf.

【衍】 leafy *adj.* 多葉的

【近】 foliage

▶ leafy ['lifɪ]

【釋】 *adj.* 葉狀的

【例】 So when the *leafy* sea dragon is swimming through these plants, predators have trouble seeing it.

【衍】 leaf *n.* 葉子

【近】 leavy

▶ lecture ['lɛktʃɚ]

【釋】 *n.* 演講

【例】 There are only three *lecture* halls in the building, one on every floor.

【衍】 lecturer *n.* 講師

【近】 speech

▶ legitimate [lɪ'dʒɪtəmɪt]

【釋】 *adj.* 合理的

【例】 You've got a *legitimate* concern, but it's understandable if you're uncomfortable asking.

【衍】 legitimatize *v.* 使合法化

【近】 reasonable

單字表 5

▶ leisure ['liʒɚ]

【釋】 *n.* 閒暇

【例】 The eel captures the fish easily and can eat it at its *leisure*.

【衍】 leisurely *adv.* 悠閒地 *adj.* 悠閒的

▶ lift [lɪft]

【釋】 *v.* 抬起

【例】 And when skunks are approached by a predator, they *lift* their tail and spray the predator with this liquid.

▶ limited ['lɪmɪtɪd]

【釋】 *adj.* 有限的

【例】 However, because resources are *limited*, only a certain number of animals of a particular species are able to survive in a given habitat.

【衍】 limit *n.* 限制 *v.* 限制 limitation *n.* 限制

▶ liquid ['lɪkwɪd]

【釋】 *n.* 液體

【例】 These aphids produce a sweet *liquid* that the ants like to eat.

【衍】 liquidity *n.* 流動性

【近】 fluid

▶ literature ['lɪtərə‚tʃur]

【釋】 *n.* 文學

【例】 This is my last semester and I've still got two required courses left to take in order to finish my *literature* degree.

【衍】 literary *adj.* 文學的

▶ lizard ['lɪzɚd]

【釋】 *n.* 蜥蜴

【例】 When the *lizard* senses these vibrations, it moves very quickly.

▶ loaf [lof]

【釋】 *n.* 遊蕩

【例】 This decrease in personal effort, especially on a simple group task, is known as social *loafing*.

【衍】 loafer *n.* 樂福鞋；遊手好閒的人

▶ lobby ['lɑbɪ]

【釋】 *n.* 大廳

【例】 I think the *lobby* at the entrance to the student center would be a great location.

▶ locomotion [ˌlokə'moʃən]

【釋】 *n.* 運動

【例】 This moving around underground is called subsurface *locomotion*.

【衍】 locomote *v.* 移動

【近】 movement

▶ locus ['lokəs]

【釋】 *n.* 關注的焦點

【例】 OK, have you ever thought about the things that happen to you and what's responsible for them? We psychologists have a term *Locus* of Control.

▶ logical ['lɑdʒɪkl]

【釋】 *adj.* 邏輯的

【例】 Students in particular have become used to relying on email and the Internet for most communication, so this is a *logical* change that will benefit everyone.

【衍】 logic *n.* 邏輯 *adj.* 邏輯的

▶ lounge [laundʒ]

【釋】 *n.* 休息室

【例】 An important additional feature of the *lounge* will be a bulletin board on the wall for posting and sharing information that may be especially useful to commuter students and their particular needs.

▶ loyal ['lɔɪəl]

【釋】 *adj.* 忠誠的

【例】 It'll already have *loyal* customers following.

【衍】 loyally *adv.* 真誠地 loyalty *n.* 忠誠

【近】 devoted

▶ lure [lur]

【釋】 *v.* 引誘

【例】 And when they get *lured* in and land on the leaf, wham! The leaf springs shut.

【近】 induce

▶ maintain [men'ten]

【釋】 *v.* 保持

【例】 Emotional intelligence helps people to behave appropriately in social situations, which allow them to *maintain* good relationships with others.

【衍】 maintenance *n.* 維護；維修
【近】 sustain

▶ **mammal** ['mæml]

【釋】 *n.* 哺乳動物
【例】 For example, the mole, a small, furry *mammal*, has really wide, super strong front feet with big claws.

▶ **manipulate** [mə'nɪpjulet]

【釋】 *v.* 操縱
【例】 Artists combine and *manipulate* these visual elements to express a message or to create a mood.
【衍】 manipulation *n.* 操縱

【近】 handle

▶ **marathon** ['mærəˌθɑn]

【釋】 *n.* 馬拉松
【例】 I don't go because I'm training for a *marathon* or anything. I just enjoy it.
【衍】 marathoner *n.* 馬拉松運動員

▶ **margarine** ['mɑrdʒərɪn]

【釋】 *n.* 人造奶油
【例】 *Margarine* is butter's substitute and you can bake equally well with either.

▶ **maximum** ['mæksəməm]

【釋】 *n.* 最大值
【例】 First, the borrowing period should be shortened to

four hours *maximum* so that more bikes would be available when students want to borrow them.

【衍】 maximization *n.* 最大化

▶ mayonnaise [ˈmeəˌnez]

【釋】 *n.* 美乃滋

【例】 Companies started using plastic containers for condiments such as ketchup, mustard and *mayonnaise*.

▶ mealtime [ˈmilˌtaɪm]

【釋】 *n.* 用餐時間

【例】 Mary Dixon, Director of the Student Life Committee, announced yesterday that beginning next semester, university cafeterias will broadcast classical music during *mealtimes*.

▶ mechanism [ˈmɛkəˌnɪzəm]

【釋】 *n.* 機制

【例】 If a predator does not recognize the meaning of this coloration and attacks, it may suffer significant discomfort or injury when its would-be prey employs its defense *mechanism*.

【衍】 mechanical *adj.* 機械的

▶ membrane [ˈmɛmbren]

【釋】 *n.* 膜

【例】 To begin with, moles have tiny eyes and these eyes are covered with a thin skin, a protective *membrane* that's actually got hair on it.

▶ merchandise ['mɝtʃənˌdaɪz]

【釋】 v. 推銷

【例】 An effective, widely used marketing practice in the entertainment industry is entertainment *merchandising*.

【衍】 merchandiser n. 商人

▶ mercury ['mɝkjərɪ]

【釋】 n. 水星

【例】 *Mercury* is the closest planet to the Sun.

【衍】 mercurial *adj.* 水 銀 的；水星的

▶ metal ['mɛtl]

【釋】 *adj.* 金屬製的

【例】 And they might decorate that nice *metal* box with beautiful pictures of some kind.

【衍】 metallic *adj.* 金屬的；含金屬的

▶ meter ['mitɚ]

【釋】 n. 公尺

【例】 Attached to the tree, sometimes 30 or 40 *meters* high, these aerial plants have access to sunlight but not to nutrients from the soil below.

▶ mice [maɪs]

【釋】 n. 老鼠（複數）

【例】 Hawks eat animals like *mice*.

【衍】 mouse *n.* 老鼠（單數）

▶ minor ['maɪnɚ]

【釋】 *adj.* 輕微的

【例】 The situation at the health center is unacceptable: you sit in a crowded waiting room for hours waiting to get treatment for *minor* ailments.

【衍】 minority *n.* 少數民族；少數派

▶ mobility [mo'bɪlətɪ]

【釋】 *n.* 移動性

【例】 But, they have a lot more *mobility* because their camouflage allows them to blend in to any environment, and because cuttlefish have shifting pigments that allow them to change color in a matter of seconds. So they can almost instantaneously match their color of their surroundings.

【衍】 mobile *adj.* 可移動的

▶ modification [ˌmɑdɪfɪ'keʃən]

【釋】 *n.* 改變

【例】 While behavior *modification* can be observed in experiments, it also occurs frequently in everyday settings, when individuals change their behavior based on what they have learned about the consequences of that behavior.

【衍】 modify *v.* 修改 modified *adj.* 改進的；修改的

▶ moisture ['mɔɪstʃɚ]

【釋】 *n.* 水分

【例】 The covering acts like a barrier that locks in *moisture*.

【衍】 moist *adj.* 潮溼的

▶ **monetary** ['mʌnɪtɛrɪ]

【釋】 *adj.* 貨幣的

【例】 A *monetary* system made it easier to make purchases.

【衍】 monetarist *adj.* 貨幣主義者

▶ **monitor** ['mɑnətə]

【釋】 *n.* 監視器

【例】 So the company can use its existing technological resources to make the *monitors*.

【衍】 monitory *adj.* 訓誡的 *n.* 告誡書

▶ **monologue** ['mɑnlˌɔg]

【釋】 *n.* 獨白

【例】 Well, to audition, you have to perform a *monologue*. You choose a small part of the play, like two or three minutes, and you perform it for the director.

【近】 soliloquy

▶ **mountainous** ['mauntnəs]

【釋】 *adj.* 多山的

【例】 And moving around in this *mountainous* environment can be challenging.

【衍】 mountain *n.* 山

▶ **muddy** ['mʌdɪ]

【釋】 *adj.* 泥濘的

【例】 Some fish have poorly developed eyes, and the water they live in can be *muddy* and dark.

【衍】 mud *v.* 泥

▶ muffin ['mʌfɪn]

【釋】 *n.* 小鬆餅

【例】 The last time I was there, the cakes and *muffins* my friends and I ordered were dry and didn't have much flavor.

▶ munch [mʌntʃ]

【釋】 *v.* 用力咀嚼

【例】 Well, like the part about how it'll help students concentrate, I mean, maybe a little snack will help the person who's eating it, but, the trouble is that it makes it hard for everyone else to concentrate cause they have to listen to someone *munching* on chips, or biting into an apple, or crinkling paper wrappers.

▶ muscle ['mʌsl]

【釋】 *n.* 肌肉

【例】 Mountain goats have a large, well-muscled chest and front-leg area, and these big, developed *muscles* in this area help them pull themselves up these near-vertical slopes, and balance in tight positions when climbing down.

【衍】 muscular *adj.* 肌肉的；肌肉發達的

▶ mustard ['mʌstɚd]

【釋】 *n.* 芥末醬

【例】 You just held the container over your food, gave it a little squeeze and out came the ketchup or *mustard*, uh, much faster and easier than having to remove a lid first.

▶ nail [nel]

【釋】 *n.* 釘子

【例】 But compared that with this: my daughter, she's six; we were building a bird house together last week, and I was showing her how to use a hammer and a *nail*.

▶ narrator [næ'retɚ]

【釋】 *n.* 敘述者

【例】 So an omniscient *narrator* provides more information and answers questions that the reader might have about the characters or the action.

【衍】 narrate *v.* 敘 述 narration *n.* 敘述

▶ narrow ['næro]

【釋】 *adj.* 狹窄的

【例】 So a *narrower* definition of money might be whatever is legal tender in a society, whatever has to be accepted as payment.

【衍】 narrowly *adv.* 仔 細 地 ； 勉強地

▶ nectar ['nɛktɚ]

【釋】 *n.* 花蜜

【例】 And on these leaves is a

sweet *nectar* that attracts insects.

【衍】 nectarous *adj.* 甘美的

▶ negative [ˈnɛɡətɪv]

【釋】 *adj.* 負面的

【例】 Sometimes companies realize that consumers may have developed a *negative* impression of a product.

【衍】 negatively *adv.* 消極地

【近】 passive

▶ nightly [ˈnaɪtlɪ]

【釋】 *adv.* 夜晚地

【例】 Currently, the campus music building—which has practice rooms students can reserve for playing instruments—closes *nightly* at nine p.m.

【衍】 night *adj.* 夜晚的 *n.* 夜晚

▶ nonliving [nɑnˈlɪvɪŋ]

【釋】 *adj.* 非生物的

【例】 Abiotic factors are *nonliving* things in the surrounding environment that can cause population changes, such as weather or sunlight.

▶ nonverbal [nɑnˈvɝbl]

【釋】 *adj.* 非言語的

【例】 *Nonverbal* language refers to human emotional expressions without involving verbal statements.

【衍】 verbal *adj.* 言語的

▶ nostril [ˈnɑstrəl]

【釋】 *n.* 鼻孔

【例】 The fulmar needs to find foods that scatter far out over the ocean, but the fulmar has a rather unusual advantage: it has tiny tubes inside the nose holes in its beak, and these special tube-shaped *nostrils* help it to pick up scent of food.

▶ notice ['notɪs]

【釋】 *v.* 注意

【例】 So, while a whale probably wouldn't *notice* one sardine, it would see a group of sardines very easily and thus be able to capture them for food.

【衍】 noted *adj.* 著名的

▶ numerous ['numərəs]

【釋】 *adj.* 許多的

【例】 Now, in the grassland of Lake Ecosystem, we'd expect to find fossils from a variety of animals, and *numerous* fossils have been found at least at these particular sites.

【近】 many, plenty

▶ nut [nʌt]

【釋】 *n.* 堅果

【例】 And it puts just one *nut* in each hole.

【衍】 nuttily *adv.* 瘋狂地；堅果般地

▶ nutrition [nuˈtrɪʃən]

【釋】 *n.* 營養

【例】 That's a big advantage because if the eel eats something big, that's a lot of food, a lot of *nutrition*.

【衍】 nutrient *adj.* 營養的

【近】 alimentation

▶ objective [əb'dʒɛktɪv]

【釋】 *n.* 目標

【例】 One *objective* of any experiment is, of course, to obtain accurate results.

【衍】 object *n.* 目標；物體 objectivity *n.* 客觀；客觀性

【近】 purpose

▶ obstacle ['ɑbstəkl]

【釋】 *n.* 障礙

【例】 And sometimes when the ants are moving toward food source, they'll encounter an *obstacle* in their path.

▶ obtain [əb'ten]

【釋】 *v.* 獲得

【例】 They use this money to *obtain* other goods and services.

【近】 acquire

▶ occasional [ə'keʒənl]

【釋】 *n.* 偶爾的

【例】 Yeah, I guess they're just making *occasional* trips to take exams or go to the library or gym or whatever.

【衍】 occasion *n.* 時機

▶ odd [ɑd]

【釋】 *adj.* 奇怪的

【例】 This often led to effects that looked *odd* from a traditional standpoint but that became hallmarks of modern architecture for precisely this reason.

【衍】 oddly *adv.* 奇妙地

▶ odor ['odə]

【釋】 *n.* 氣味

【例】 Now, this highly-developed sense of smell is especially important because the fulmar's main source of food, plankton, are tiny organisms that are hard to see, but they give off a very sharp, distinctive *odor,* so when fulmars are flying around looking for food, they may not be able to see them, but they can find the plankton by smelling them even from far away.

【衍】 odorless *adj.* 沒有氣味的

【近】 smell

▶ offer ['ɔfə]

【釋】 *v.* 提供

【例】 I mean it's really nice of them to *offer.*

【衍】 offering *n.* 提供；祭品

【近】 provide

▶ official [ə'fɪʃəl]

【釋】 *n.* 行政官員

【例】 A university *official* announced plans to spend $2 million to build a new stadium, commenting that a new stadium would help the university achieve its goal of attracting more top students.

【衍】 officially *adj.* 正式地

▶ old-fashioned ['old͵fæʃənd]

【釋】 *adj.* 過時的

【例】 Our technology was advanced but the outside design looked really *old-fashioned*.

【近】 ancient

▶ omelet ['ɑmlət]

【釋】 *n.* 煎蛋捲

【例】 Let's say maybe on a cold morning, in that case, which is going to be better for you, a bowl of cold cereal or a nice warm *omelet*? It's obvious.

▶ omniscient [ɑm'nɪʃənt]

【釋】 *adj.* 無所不知的

【例】 So an *omniscient* narrator provides more information and answers questions that the reader might have about the characters or the action.

【衍】 omniscience *n.* 全知;上帝

▶ online ['ɑn͵laɪn]

【釋】 *adj.* 線上的

【例】 We do it *online*. That's cool.

▶ oppose [ə'poz]

【釋】 *v.* 反對

【例】 We should all *oppose* this plan.

【衍】 opposed *adj.* 相反的;敵對的

【近】 object

▶ opposite ['ɑpəzɪt]

【釋】 *adj.* 相反的

【例】 I don't know what students they asked, but I know a lot of people who feel just the *opposite*.

【衍】 oppositive *adj.* 反 對 的 ; 相反的

【近】 contrary

▶ optimal ['ɑptəml]

【釋】 *adj.* 最優的

【例】 This energy-efficient approach to obtaining food is known as *optimal* foraging.

【衍】 optimum *adj.* 最適宜的

▶ option ['ɑpʃən]

【釋】 *n.* 選擇

【例】 But there is one other *option*.

【衍】 optional *adj.* 可選擇的

【近】 choice

▶ oral ['ɔrəl]

【釋】 *adj.* 口頭的

【例】 The final project for this course will be an *oral* presentation.

【衍】 orally *adv.* 口頭上地

【近】 verbal

▶ orchestra ['ɔrkɪstrə]

【釋】 *n.* 樂隊

【例】 And we really could use more time slots, especially just before the big concerts: the winter concert and the spring concert, because everybody from all sections of the *orchestra* needs to practice then.

▶ ordinary [ˈɔrdnɛrɪ]

【釋】 *adj.* 日常的

【例】 Let's take an everyday example—an *ordinary* round
plate like you'd find in a
kitchen.

【近】 general

▶ organic [ɔrˈɡænɪk]

【釋】 *adj.* 有機的

【例】 First let's look at one way
that lakes can disappear
naturally, and that is, by
gradually getting filled in
with *organic* sediment.

【衍】 organism *n.* 有機體

▶ organism [ˈɔrɡənɪzəm]

【釋】 *n.* 有機體

【例】 Rocks near the Earth's surface are directly exposed to
elements in the environment
such as air and water, and
also to conditions such as
temperature change as well
as to living *organism*.

【衍】 organic *adj.* 有機的

▶ organize [ˈɔrɡənˌaɪz]

【釋】 *v.* 組織

【例】 The program will also be
organized so that individual students can arrange to
work with tutors majoring
in their own chosen field of
study.

【衍】 organized *adj.* 有組織的
organization *n.* 組織

▶ orientation [ˌɔrɪɛnˈteʃən]

【釋】 *n.* 培訓

【例】 Madison University is making a change to the *orientation* program for first-year students.

【衍】 orient *v.* 使適應 *n.* 東方 oriented *adj.* 定向的

▶ original [ə'rɪdʒənl]

【釋】 *adj.* 最初的

【例】 The *original* purpose for the behavior may have disappeared long ago, even thousands of years before.

【衍】 origin *n.* 起源

【近】 initial

▶ outcome ['aut͵kʌm]

【釋】 *n.* 結果

【例】 The experimenter effect occurs when a researcher's expectations affect the *outcome* of the experiment.

【近】 result

▶ outer ['autɚ]

【釋】 *adj.* 外部的

【例】 It takes off the *outer* shell and cleans it.

【衍】 out *adj.* 外面的 *adv.* 在外

【近】 outside, external

▶ outsider [aut'saɪdɚ]

【釋】 *n.* 外人

【例】 Because they do not learn conventional artistic techniques from teachers or other artists, *outsider* artists must invent their own ways of doing things.

【衍】 outside *adj.* 外面的 *adv.* 在外

▶ outweigh [aut'we]

【釋】 *v.* 比……重要

【例】 This special feature may *outweigh* the customer's concern.

▶ oval ['ovl]

【釋】 *n.* 橢圓形

【例】 Suppose you tilt the plate to a different angle, to a horizontal position, like you're planning to put food on it, still a perfect circle? No! The circle is now stretched out, flattened into an *oval*.

【衍】 ovate *adj.* 卵圓形的

▶ overall [ˌovɚˈɔl]

【釋】 *adv.* 總的來說

【例】 *Overall*, a bird's eyes are extremely important for its survival.

▶ overcrowded [ˌovəˈkraudɪd]

【釋】 *adj.* 過度擁擠的

【例】 The money saved by eliminating the bus service will be used to expand the *overcrowded* student parking lots.

【衍】 crowded *adj.* 擁擠的

▶ overlap [ovɚˈlæp]

【釋】 *v.* 重疊

【例】 The leaves are slightly *overlapping* and are tightly rolled into a kind of cone shape or a funnel shape.

▶ owl [aul]

【釋】 *n.* 貓頭鷹

【例】 A bird like the Arctic snowy *owl,* for example, has feathers on its body the way other birds do.

【衍】 owlish *adj.* 貓頭鷹般的; 看似聰明的;面孔嚴肅的

▶ oxygen ['ɑksədʒən]

【釋】 *n.* 氧氣

【例】 Another environmental condition is lack of *oxygen.*

【衍】 oxygenize *v.* 使氧化

▶ pain [pen]

【釋】 *n.* 疼痛

【例】 The Chinese practice using needles to cure disease or relieve *pain.*

【衍】 painful *adj.* 痛苦的 pain-less *adj.* 無痛的

【近】 hurt

單字表 6

▶ paper ['pepɚ]

【釋】 *n.* 論文

【例】 I'll read a book or bring my laptop computer and work on a *paper* for class.

【衍】 papery *adj.* 薄的；像紙的

【近】 thesis

▶ paralyze ['pærə͵laɪz]

【釋】 *v.* 使癱瘓

【例】 The electric current that it sends out shocks the smaller fish and *paralyzes* it.

【衍】 paralyzed *adj.* 癱瘓的

▶ parrot ['pærət]

【釋】 *n.* 鸚鵡

【例】 Now, the great green macaw is a beautiful bird, a fairly large-sized *parrot* known for its colorful feathers, gorgeous green feathers with some red and blue feathers, too.

▶ participate [pɑr'tɪsə͵peɪt]

【釋】 *v.* 參與

【例】 That gave all the students a chance to *participate* which helped everyone get more out of the discussion.

【衍】 participation *n.* 參與

【近】 take part in

▶ particular [pɚ'tɪkjəlɚ]

【釋】 *adj.* 特定的

【例】 An artist chooses certain colors to evoke a *particular* mood and make powerful statements.

【衍】 particularly *adv.* 特別地

▶ part-time [ˌpɑrt'taɪm]

【釋】 *adj.* 兼職的

【例】 If money is the problem, they could hire a *part-time* professor.

▶ passive ['pæsɪv]

【釋】 *adj.* 被動的

【例】 *Passive* attention requires no effort because it happens naturally.

【衍】 passively *adv.* 被動地

【近】 negative

▶ pavement ['pevmənt]

【釋】 *n.* 人行道

【例】 *Pavement* would solve this problem.

【近】 sidewalk, footpath

▶ payment ['pemənt]

【釋】 *n.* 付款

【例】 The taxi driver must accept coins or bills as *payment* for a taxi ride.

【衍】 pay *v.* 支付 payer *n.* 付款人

▶ peak [pik]

【釋】 *n.* 山峰

【例】 It's got *peaks* and valleys, vegetation, rocky areas, and some sea animals have developed permanent colors or shapes to resemble these environmental features.

【衍】 peaky *adj.* 尖峰的；憔悴的

▶ peanut ['pinʌt]

【釋】 *n.* 花生

【例】 There's a large tropical insect called the *Peanut* Bug.

▶ peck [pɛk]

【釋】 *v.* 啄食

【例】 And what the chickens do is walking around inside the house and *pecking* at the soil.

【衍】 pecker *n.* 啄木鳥；穿孔器

▶ peel [pil]

【釋】 *v.* 去皮

【例】 They were simply asked to peel potatoes, and to *peel* as many potatoes as possible in a given amount of time.

▶ perceive [pɚ'siv]

【釋】 *v.* 理解

【例】 Do you conclude the plate had actually changed shape, or that it's a different object, not the same plate? Of course not! It looks different, but we *perceive* it as still being the same.

【衍】 perception *n.* 知覺；感知

▶ perceptual [pɚ'sɛptʃuəl]

【釋】 *adj.* 知覺的

【例】 This is what is known as *perceptual* constancy.

【衍】 perception *n.* 知覺；感知 perceive *v.* 理解

【近】 sensory

▶ perfectly ['pɜ-fɪktlɪ]

【釋】 *adv.* 完美地

【例】 In order to sell more products, advertisers will often
try to make us believe that a
product will meet our needs
or desires *perfectly,* even if
it's not true.

【衍】 perfect *adj.* 完美的

▶ performance [pɚ-'fɔrməns]

【釋】 *n.* 表演

【例】 The choir's new director
feels that entering singing
competitions will make the
quality of the choir's *performance* even better than it is
now.

【衍】 perform *v.* 執行；完成；演奏

▶ period ['pɪrɪəd]

【釋】 *n.* 時期

【例】 This *period* of transition,
when people are adjusting
to technological change, is
known as cultural lag.

【衍】 periodical *n.* 期刊；雜誌
adj. 定期的

▶ persuade [pɚ-'swed]

【釋】 *v.* 說服

【例】 In this way, companies can
persuade consumers to purchase a product despite its
drawbacks.

【衍】 persuasive *adj.* 有說服力的

【近】 convince

▶ phenomenon [fə'nɑmɪnən]

【釋】 *n.* 現象

【例】 Now a study was done that illustrated this *phenomenon*.

【衍】 phenomenal *adj.* 現象的；顯著的

▶ philosophy [fə'lɑsəfɪ]

【釋】 *n.* 哲學

【例】 So, lots of people in the US have realized that acupuncture is effective, but few of them fully understand or have committed themselves to the *philosophy* behind acupuncture.

【衍】 philosopher *n.* 哲學家

▶ pigment ['pɪgmənt]

【釋】 *n.* 色素

【例】 But, they have a lot more mobility because their camouflage allows them to blend in to any environment, and because cuttlefish have shifting *pigments* that allow them to change color in a matter of seconds. So they can almost instantaneously match their color of their surroundings.

▶ plain [plen]

【釋】 *adj.* 普通的

【例】 Instead of selling their cookies in a *plain* cardboard box, they might sell them in a nice metal box.

【衍】 plainly *adv.* 平坦地；明白地；樸素地

▶ planet ['plænɪt]

【釋】 *n.* 行星

【例】 Mercury is the closest *planet* to the Sun.

【衍】 planetary *adj.* 行星的

▶ plastic ['plæstɪk]

【釋】 *adj.* 塑膠的

【例】 Companies started using *plastic* containers for condiments such as ketchup, mustard and mayonnaise.

【衍】 plasticity *n.* 塑性；可塑性；適應性

▶ plate [plet]

【釋】 *n.* 盤子

【例】 Let's take an everyday example—an ordinary round *plate* like you'd find in a kitchen.

【衍】 platy *adj.* 板狀的；扁平狀的

【近】 dish

▶ platform ['plæt‚fɔrm]

【釋】 *n.* 平臺

【例】 For example, various species known as epiphytes use a host plant as a *platform* for growth.

▶ plenty ['plɛntɪ]

【釋】 *n.* 很多

【例】 When you are driving along a highway, you see *plenty* of billboards, road side advertisements.

【衍】 plentiful *adj.* 豐富的；許多的

【近】 abundance

▶ **pollen** ['pɑlən]

【釋】 *n.* 花粉

【例】 Mites live in tropical climates and feed on nectar and *pollen* in flowers.

【衍】 pollenate *v.* 給……授花粉

▶ **pop** [pɑp]

【釋】 *adj.* 流行的

【例】 Now during TV shows that young people watch, shows with *pop* music or teen serials create a commercial that emphasizes how fun the phone is.

【衍】 popular *adj.* 流行的

▶ **portable** ['pɔrtəbl]

【釋】 *adj.* 行動式的

【例】 And a salesperson's showing her a *portable* laptop computer.

【衍】 portability *n.* 可攜帶性

▶ **poster** ['postɚ]

【釋】 *n.* 海報

【例】 I had seen the *poster* for the jazz festival in Monterey.

【衍】 post *v.* 張 貼；公 佈 *n.* 郵件；職位

▶ **potential** [pə'tɛnʃl]

【釋】 *adj.* 潛在的

【例】 The first time the animals would see a human being, they'd instinctively react by making a sharp barking and jumping up and down, essentially warning or alerting other prairie dogs that are nearby of this *potential* threat.

【衍】 potentially *adv.* 可 能 地 ；潛 在 地 potentiality *n.* 潛力；可能性

【近】 underlying

▶ prairie ['prɛrɪ]

【釋】 *n.* 草原

【例】 Let's assume that some *prairie* dogs happen to live in an area where human beings frequently come and go.

▶ predator ['prɛdətɚ]

【釋】 *n.* 捕食者

【例】 And that surprises the *predator* and gives the peanut bug a chance to get away.

【衍】 predatory *adj.* 掠奪的 predation *n.* 捕食；掠奪

▶ predictable [prɪ'dɪktəbl]

【釋】 *adj.* 可預測的

【例】 This familiar place should have a series of landmarks or locations within it that we can imagine walking past in a *predictable,* logical order.

【衍】 predict *v.* 預言；預測 prediction *n.* 預言；預報

【近】 divinable

▶ preference ['prɛfərəns]

【釋】 *n.* 偏愛

【例】 People tend to develop a *preference* for things they have previously encoun-

tered, things they are familiar with.

【衍】 preferred *adj.* 優 先 的；
首選的

▶ preoccupied [pri'ɑkjə,paɪd]

【釋】 *adj.* 全神貫注的

【例】 And everyone'll be so *preoccupied* by then.

【衍】 preoccupy *v.* 迷 住；使 全
神貫注 preoccupation *n.* 全
神貫注；當務之急

【近】 concentrated

▶ presence ['prɛzns]

【釋】 *n.* 存在

【例】 In some cases, these animals have distinct coloring
that signals predators of the
presence of such defenses.

【衍】 present *v.* 提出；呈現；贈送

【近】 existence

▶ present [prɪ'zɛnt]

【釋1】 *n.* 現在

【例】 At *present*, students are
required to meet with their
academic advisors before
the beginning of every semester.

【衍】 presence *n.* 存 在； 出
席；參加

【釋2】 *adj.* 現在的

【例】 Once a pronghorn starts
running, zoom! None of its
present predators, like the
bobcat or the coyote, can
even hope to catch up with
it.

【釋3】 *v.* 呈現

【例】 The partners will orally *present* their research to the class during the last two weeks of classes.

▶ preserve [prɪˈzɝv]

【釋】 *v.* 儲存

【例】 This preparation may in some way help *preserve* the nut and or may make it easier to eat later on.

【衍】 preservation *n.* 儲存；保留

【近】 save, maintain

▶ president [ˈprɛzɪdənt]

【釋】 *n.* 校長

【例】 I mean, a lot of people give speeches, such as students, professors, administrators, and the *president* of the university.

【衍】 presidential *adj.* 總統的；統轄的

【近】 principal

▶ press [prɛs]

【釋】 *v.* 按

【例】 I found that I still knew where to *press* my fingers to play the right notes.

【衍】 pressing *adj.* 緊迫的；急切的

▶ previous [ˈprivɪəs]

【釋】 *adj.* 以前的

【例】 One explanation is that we remember something better if we already have some previous knowledge about it, some *previous* understanding of it.

【衍】 previously *adv.* 預先

▶ primacy ['praɪməsɪ]

【釋】 *n.* 首位

【例】 This tendency is called the *primacy* effect.

【衍】 primary *adj.* 主要的

▶ principle ['prɪnsəpl]

【釋】 *n.* 原則

【例】 Social psychologists refer to this tendency as the familiarity *principle*.

【衍】 principled *adj.* 有原則的；有操守的

▶ procedural [prə'sidʒərəl]

【釋】 *adj.* 程式上的

【例】 These memories of performing particular actions are called *procedural* memories.

【衍】 procedure *n.* 程式；手續

▶ produce [prə'dus]

【釋】 *v.* 產生

【例】 What I want to talk about now is a special ability some fish have—the ability to *produce* electricity in their bodies.

【衍】 production *n.* 成果；產品；生產 productive *adj.* 多產的；富有成效的

▶ product ['prɑdʌkt]

【釋】 *n.* 產品

【例】 Attractive containers like that can make a *product* much more appealing to consumers.

【衍】 production *n.* 成果；產品；生產 productive *adj.* 多產的；富有成效的

▶ programming ['progræmɪŋ]

【釋】 n. 節目

【例】 Changes would include an expansion of the station's broadcasting range, which would allow the radio's *programming* to reach nearby towns.

【衍】 program *n.* 程式；計劃 programmer *n.* 程式員

▶ prolong [prə'lɔŋ]

【釋】 v. 持續

【例】 It doesn't rust, even with *prolonged* exposure to water.

【衍】 prolonged *adj.* 延長的；持續很久的

▶ proposal [prə'pozl]

【釋】 n. 提議

【例】 I don't like his *proposal*.

【衍】 propose *v.* 建議；打算；求婚

▶ propose [prə'poz]

【釋】 v. 建議

【例】 I *propose* that the university close the campus coffeehouse.

【衍】 proposal *n.* 提議

▶ protein ['protin]

【釋】 n. 蛋白質

【例】 So their food needs to be rich in *protein*.

▶ psychologist [saɪ'kɑlədʒɪst]

【釋】 n. 心理學家

【例】 In everyday life, when people speak of memory, they are almost always speaking about what *psychologists* would call explicit memories.

【衍】 psychology *n.* 心理學 psychological *adj.* 心理學的

▶ pump [pʌmp]

【釋】 *v.* 抽水

【例】 And sometimes to get that water, they *pump* that water out of a nearby lake.

▶ pursue [pɚ'su]

【釋】 *v.* 追求

【例】 The school feels that this will give students who are studying cooking and food preparation valuable experience that will help them later, when they *pursue* careers.

【衍】 pursuit *n.* 追趕;追求;職業

▶ quiz [kwɪz]

【釋】 *n.* 考試

【例】 We are not getting much studying done, and none of us did very well on your last *quiz*.

【近】 test, exam

▶ rack [ræk]

【釋】 *n.* 機架

【例】 I think the university should remove these bikes from the *racks* and dispose of them.

【衍】 racking *adj.* 拷問的;折磨人的

▶ radiate ['redɪet]

【釋】 *v.* 輻射

【例】 It absorbs and *radiates* heat.

【衍】 radiation *n.* 輻射

▶ rainforest ['renˌfɔrɪst]

【釋】 *n.* 雨林

【例】 The macaw lives in the South American rainforest, in a part of the *rainforest* where a lot of trees have been cut down, trees that the macaw relies on for its food and nesting.

▶ range [rendʒ]

【釋】 *n.* 範圍

【例】 I mean, the *range* of the station now is basically limited to the campus.

【近】 extent

▶ rapidly ['ræpɪdlɪ]

【釋】 *adv.* 迅速地

【例】 OK, lakes can also disappear, pretty *rapidly* sometimes, as a result of human activities.

【衍】 rapid *adj.* 迅速的

【近】 quickly

▶ react [ri'ækt]

【釋】 *v.* 反應

【例】 They'd instinctively *react* by making a sharp barking sound.

【衍】 reaction *n.* 反應；反作用

▶ realistically [ˌriə'lɪstɪklɪ]

【釋】 *adv.* 逼真地

【例】 Before the camera, it was extremely difficult to *realistically* depict a moving object in a painting.

【衍】 realistic *adj.* 現實的；逼真的

▶ receive [rɪ'siv]

【釋】 v. 接受

【例】 Oh, you could have someone else to *receive* the
award for you.

【衍】 reception *n.* 接收；招待會

【近】 accept

▶ recent ['risnt]

【釋】 *adj.* 最近的

【例】 However, more *recent*
trends in advertising have
turned toward target mar-
keting.

【衍】 recently *adv.* 最近

【近】 current

▶ receptacle [rɪ'sɛptəkl]

【釋】 *n.* 容器

【例】 Anyway, as I mentioned,
the arrangement of the
leaves forms a kind of
receptacle or bowl at the
base.

【近】 container

▶ recollection [ˌrɛkə'lɛkʃən]

【釋】 *n.* 回憶

【例】 An explicit memory is a
conscious or intentional
recollection, usually of
facts, names, events, or
other things that a person
can state or declare.

【衍】 recollect *v.* 回憶；想起

【近】 memory, recall

▶ recommend [ˌrɛkə'mɛnd]

【釋】 *v.* 推薦

【例】 I *recommend* this action

because, first of all, they will not be missed by anyone, since they apparently have been forgotten by their owners.

【衍】 recommendation *n.* 推薦

▶ recreation [ˌrɛkrɪˈeʃən]

【釋】 *n.* 娛樂

【例】 The university administration today announced a $25 increase in the student fee for using the campus *recreation* center.

【衍】 recreational *adj.* 娛樂的

【近】 entertainment

▶ refer [rɪˈfɝ]

【釋】 *v.* 提到，談到

【例】 This tendency is often *referred* to as the comfort zone bias.

【衍】 reference *n.* 參照

▶ reference [ˈrɛfərəns]

【釋】 *n.* 參照

【例】 Groups of people whom we admire and whose behavior and attitudes we tend to imitate are known as *reference* groups.

【衍】 refer *v.* 提到，談到

▶ refill [ˌriˈfɪl]

【釋】 *v.* 填滿

【例】 Now that's OK if the lake is continually being *refilled* with rainwater or with water from streams that run into the lake. But if there isn't enough rainwater or stream

water to replace the water
the farmers take out of the
lake, the lake will eventually dry up.

▶ refute [rɪ'fjut]

【釋】 *n.* 反駁

【例】 One way in which they
can resolve this problem
is by using an advertising
technique known as *re-*
fute-and-persuade.

【衍】 refutation *n.* 反駁；駁斥

【近】 disprove

▶ rehearsal [rɪ'hɝsl]

【釋】 *n.* 排練

【例】 I'm afraid I forgot tonight
I've got a music *rehearsal*
for the band I'm in.

【衍】 rehearse *v.* 排練

▶ rehearse [rɪ'hɝs]

【釋】 *v.* 排練

【例】 I mean, right now, we don't
rehearse more than once a
week.

【衍】 rehearsal *n.* 排練

▶ reinterpret [ˌriɪn'tɝprɪt]

【釋】 *v.* 重新解釋

【例】 I *reinterpreted* my situation.

▶ relatively ['rɛlətɪvlɪ]

【釋】 *adv.* 相對地

【例】 Unlike the larger grey wolves
that live in warmer climates,
Arctic wolves have *relatively*
small, compact bodies that ef-
ficiently retain heat.

【衍】 relative *adj.* 相 對 的 ； 有 關係的

【近】 comparatively

▶ reliability [rɪˌlaɪə'bɪlətɪ]

【釋】 *n.* 可靠性

【例】 So *reliability* is important but it's not gonna be the deciding factor.

【衍】 reliable *adj.* 可靠的

【近】 dependability

▶ relieve [rɪ'liv]

【釋】 *v.* 緩解

【例】 When will you *relieve* me of the burden?

▶ remain [rɪ'men]

【釋】 *v.* 保持

【例】 In spite of this, even as conditions change and we see objects differently, we still recognize that they *remain* the same.

▶ renovate ['rɛnəvet]

【釋】 *v.* 改造

【例】 In an effort to counteract the trend, the college has announced a plan to *renovate* its on-campus housing.

【衍】 renovation *n.* 翻新 ； 改造

▶ renovation [ˌrɛnə'veʃən]

【釋】 *n.* 翻新

【例】 The advertisement is irrelevant or useless, for instance, a piece of mail I got advertising a kitchen *renovation* service.

【衍】 renovate *v.* 翻新 ； 改造

▶ rent [rɛnt]

【釋】 *v.* 租

【例】 That's why I was going to *rent* the van.

【衍】 rental *adj.* 租賃的 *n.* 租金 renter *n.* 承租人；房東

【近】 lease

▶ represent [ˌrɛprɪ'zɛnt]

【釋】 *v.* 代表

【例】 It gives children a safe way to explore certain urges and desires they have, but ones that don't *represent* typically acceptable behavior.

【衍】 representative *adj.* 有代表性的 *n.* 代表

【近】 stand for

▶ repulsive [rɪ'pʌlsɪv]

【釋】 *adj.* 令人厭惡的

【例】 That's very unpleasant for the wolf because it's now covered with this *repulsive*, foul-smelling liquid.

【衍】 repulse *v.* 拒絕；擊退

▶ reputation [ˌrɛpju'teʃən]

【釋】 *n.* 名聲

【例】 We don't want to get a *reputation* for publishing low-quality work.

【衍】 reputable *adj.* 聲譽好的

【近】 fame

▶ reschedule [ˌri'skɛdʒul]

【釋】 *v.* 重新安排

【例】 Yeah, she'd probably let me *reschedule*.

▶ resist [rɪ'zɪst]

【釋】 *v.* 抵制

【例】 Cultures tend to *resist* ideas
that seem to foreign, too
different from their own beliefs and values.

單字表 7

▶ resolve [rɪ'zɑlv]

【釋】 *v.* 解決

【例】 People experiencing cognitive dissonance often do not want to change the way they are acting, so they *resolve* the contradictory situation in another way.

【衍】 resolution *n.* 決議；決心；解決

【近】 solve

▶ restoration [ˌrɛstə'reʃən]

【釋】 *n.* 恢復；還原

【例】 They're old newspapers, and they were in pretty bad shape, so the library sent them out for repairs, like, *restoration* work.

【衍】 restore *v.* 恢復；還原

【近】 recovery

▶ restore [rɪ'stɔr]

【釋】 *v.* 恢復；還原

【例】 When individuals feel that their actions are being unfairly limited, they often attempt to *restore* freedom by directly contradicting or opposing the rule of regulation that threatened their freedom.

【衍】 restoration *n.* 恢復；還原

▶ restriction [rɪ'strɪkʃən]

【釋】 *n.* 限制

【例】 But, people found out about the upcoming *restriction* and got upset.

【衍】 restrict *v.* 限制；約束

【近】 limitation

▶ reunion [ri'junjən]

【釋】 *n.* 團聚

【例】 But there's a family *reunion* this weekend.

▶ reveal [rɪ'vil]

【釋】 *v.* 暴露

【例】 When approached by a predator, the animal suddenly *reveals* the area of bright color; this unexpected display of color startles or confuses the predator and provides the would-be-prey with an opportunity to escape.

【近】 expose

▶ revise [rɪ'vaɪz]

【釋】 *v.* 修改

【例】 So are you gonna stay around to *revise* the report? I could.

【衍】 revision *n.* 修正；複習；修訂本

▶ ridiculous [rɪ'dɪkjələs]

【釋】 *adj.* 荒謬的

【例】 Do you believe any of this? It's *ridiculous*.

【衍】 ridiculously *adv.* 可笑地

▶ ritualization [ˌrɪtʃuəlaɪ'zeʃən]

【釋】 *n.* 儀式化

【例】 Socialbiologists believe that some communicative behavior in animals is developed through a process called *ritualization*.

【衍】 ritualize *v.* 使儀式化

▶ ritualize [ˈrɪtʃuəlaɪz]

【釋】 *v.* 使儀式化

【例】 Once a behavior is *ritual-ized*, it becomes a form of communication; therefore, if an animal engages in this behavior, other animals will be able to interpret the meaning or the behavior quickly and respond appro-priately.

【衍】 ritualization *n.* 儀式化

▶ Roman [ˈromən]

【釋】 *adj.* 羅馬的

【例】 But *Roman* cities, on the other hand, grew much larger.

▶ roof [ruf]

【釋】 *n.* 屋頂

【例】 This little house has four walls and a *roof*.

【衍】 roofed *adj.* 有屋頂的

【近】 housetop

▶ root [rut]

【釋】 *n.* 根

【例】 And its *root* will grow down into the rock.

【衍】 rooted *adj.* 根深蒂固的；生根的

▶ rough [rʌf]

【釋】 *adj.* 粗糙的

【例】 Oh, that's *rough*.

【衍】 roughly *adv.* 粗糙地

【近】 crude

▶ **roughness** [ˈrʌfnɪs]

【釋】 *n.* 粗糙度

【例】 By texture I mean surface quality or feel of the work, its smoothness or *roughness* or softness.

【衍】 roughly *adv.* 粗糙地

▶ **route** [rut]

【釋】 *n.* 路線

【例】 But I think the problem is the *route's* out-of-date.

▶ **row** [ro]

【釋】 *n.* 一排

【例】 Now, from up close, from the front row, I appear to be relatively big, bigger than if you're in the last row, right? But let's say you're sitting in the front *row* today and tomorrow you're sitting in the back row.

▶ **rubbery** [ˈrʌbərɪ]

【釋】 *adj.* 橡膠的

【例】 And the back parts of their feet have special round, *rubbery* pads that help them grip the surface of the rock or ice.

【衍】 rubber *n.* 橡膠 *adj.* 橡膠製成的

▶ **rural** [ˈrurəl]

【釋】 *adj.* 農村的

【例】 So the factory would hire a lot of *rural* workers who would then move from the country side to the village.

【衍】 rurally *adv.* 鄉下地

【近】 country

 Russian ['rʌʃən]

【釋】 *adj.* 俄國的

【例】 So I signed up to take a *Russian* course online over the summer, because I'm hoping to take a trip to Russia at some point.

【衍】 Russia *n.* 俄羅斯

▶ rusty ['rʌstɪ]

【釋】 *n.* 生疏的

【例】 I am a little *rusty.*

【衍】 rust *n.* 鏽 *v.* 生鏽

▶ saturate ['sætʃəˌret]

【釋】 *v.* 使飽和

【例】 But succulent plants have a spread-out and shallow root system that can quickly pull in water from the top inch of soil, though the soil has to be *saturated,* since succulents aren't good at absorbing water from soil that's only a little moist.

【衍】 saturated *adj.* 飽 和 的； 滲透的

▶ sauce [sɔs]

【釋】 *n.* 醬

【例】 Well, I wore my white shirt to dinner and I spilt spaghetti *sauce* all over it.

▶ scarce [skɛrs]

【釋】 *adj.* 缺乏的

【例】 Later, at a time when food is *scarce,* the hoarders return to these hiding places and recover the food.

【衍】 scarcely *adv.* 幾乎不

【近】 rare

▶ scatter ['skætɚ]

【釋】 *n.* 分散

【例】 Some types of hoarders engage in *scatter* hoarding.

【衍】 scattered *adj.* 分散的

▶ scene [sin]

【釋】 *n.* 場面

【例】 We were supposed to film the final *scene* today, but it's raining.

▶ scent [sɛnt]

【釋】 *n.* 氣味

【例】 Producing heat serves two purposes: it magnifies the *scent* of the flower and it helps the beetles maintain their body temperature.

【衍】 scented *adj.* 有香味的；有氣味的

【近】 smell

▶ schedule ['skɛdʒul]

【釋】 *v.* 安排

【例】 And as for *scheduling* meetings, I've never had that kind of trouble.

【衍】 scheduled *adj.* 預定的；已排日程的

▶ scheme [skim]

【釋】 *n.* 方案

【例】 One of the reasons his *scheme* has been so widely accepted is because of his sample size.

【近】 plan

▶ scholarship ['skɑlɚʃɪp]

【釋】 n. 獎學金

【例】 Well, it's a success! They are making a lot of money out of commercials and they are using it to offer more *scholarships* and to help fund projects to reno-vate the facilities of other programs.

【衍】 scholar n. 學者

▶ scoop [skup]

【釋】 v. 舀取

【例】 And then you had to either pour the ketchup or mustard on your food which could be messy or *scoop* it out with spoon.

【衍】 scoopful n. 滿滿的一勺子

▶ scope [skop]

【釋】 n. 範圍

【例】 Businesses that perform services or carry out proj-ects for clients generally come to an agreement with their clients about the extent or *scope* of a project before beginning the project.

【近】 extent

▶ scream [skrim]

【釋】 v. 尖叫

【例】 What do you think he's going to start doing when he wants something from Mom? He'll probably cry and *scream*, right?

【衍】 screaming n. 尖叫聲 adj.

尖叫的

▶ screw [skru]

【釋】 v. 擰緊

【例】 In the past, these products came in glass containers with lids you had to *screw* off.

【衍】 screwy *adj.* 古怪的

▶ sculptor ['skʌlptɚ]

【釋】 *n.* 雕塑家

【例】 Yeah! At least a few painting teachers are also great *sculptors*.

【衍】 sculpture *n.* 雕塑

▶ sculpture ['skʌlptʃɚ]

【釋】 *n.* 雕塑

【例】 The administration has an-nounced plans to acquire a new *sculpture* for campus.

【衍】 sculptor *n.* 雕塑家

▶ seaweed ['siˌwid]

【釋】 *n.* 海藻

【例】 It's called a damselfish that likes to eat a special kind of *seaweed*.

▶ secrete [sɪ'krit]

【釋】 v. 分泌

【例】 For example, some frogs *secrete* a substance through their skin, a fatty substance that they rub off over their skin using their hands and feet, which creates a waxy layer all around their bodies that's almost completely water-tight.

【衍】 secretory *adj.* 分泌的

▶ sediment [sɛdəmənt]

【釋】 *n.* 沉積物

【例】 In the normal water phase the remaining phosphorus makes its way, settles to the bottom of the ocean and gets mixed into the ocean *sediments*.

【衍】 sedimentary *adj.* 沉澱的

▶ seek [sik]

【釋】 *v.* 尋找

【例】 Beetles will *seek* out these trees because the trees are dead.

▶ selective [sɪ'lɛktɪv]

【釋】 *adj.* 挑剔的

【例】 Well, maybe we're being too *selective*.

【衍】 select *v.* 挑選

▶ seller ['sɛlɚ]

【釋】 *n.* 賣家

【例】 The *seller* of a product finds a way to signal or demon-strate, to the buyer that the product is high-quality.

【衍】 sell *v.* 銷售

【近】 salesman

▶ seminar ['sɛmə,nɑr]

【釋】 *n.* 研討會

【例】 Currently, all of the *sem-inar* classes in the history department are three hours long.

【近】 forum

▶ semester [sə'mɛstɚ]

【釋】 *n.* 學期

【例】 Does this mean you'll be living by yourself next *semester*?

【衍】 semiannual *adj.* 半年一次的

【近】 session

▶ senior ['sinɪɚ]

【釋】 *adj.* 高級的

【例】 There were a few *senior* managers there who didn't support the design change.

【衍】 seniority *n.* 長輩

【近】 advanced

▶ sense [sɛns]

【釋】 *n.* 感覺

【例】 They missed the *sense* of personal connection they got from meeting someone.

【衍】 sensible *adj.* 明智的；能感覺到的

▶ sensitive ['sɛnsətɪv]

【釋】 *adj.* 敏感的

【例】 So the eyes, the mole's *sensitive* parts, are protected.

【衍】 sensible *adj.* 明智的；能感覺到的

▶ separate ['sɛpəˌret]

【釋1】 *v.* 分開

【例】 It is impossible to *separate* belief from emotion.

【衍】 separation *n.* 分開

【釋2】 *adj.* 單獨的

【例】 While some farmers treat the cultivation of their

animals and plants as two *separate* activities, others integrate the two so that they work together.

▶ sequence ['sikwəns]

【釋】 *n.* 順序

【例】 The next thing you do is assign one planet to each of your landmarks in *sequence*.

【衍】 sequential *adj.* 連續的

【近】 order

▶ serial ['sɪrɪəl]

【釋】 *n.* 電視連續劇

【例】 Now during TV shows that young people watch, shows with pop music or teen *serials* create a commercial that emphasizes how fun the phone is.

【衍】 serially *adv.* 連 續 地；連載地

【近】 TV series

▶ series ['sɪriz]

【釋】 *n.* 系列

【例】 And before the secrets are revealed to the main characters, the plot of the play proceeds as a *series* of sort of up and down moments.

【衍】 serially *adv.* 連 續 地；連載地

▶ session ['sɛʃən]

【釋】 *n.* 課程

【例】 My students have a test next week so tomorrow's class is the review *session*.

▶ shady ['ʃedɪ]

【釋】 *adj.* 陰暗的

【例】 In rain forests, the canopy produced by the upper layer of branches may be so dense that few plants can grow on the *shady* ground below.

【衍】 shade *n.* 樹蔭；陰影

▶ shape [ʃep]

【釋】 *n.* 形狀

【例】 An object viewed from one angle presents a different *shape* to our eyes than when viewed from another angle; similarly, as the distance from which we view an object changes, the object will appear larger or smaller.

【衍】 shaped *adj.* 合適的；呈某種形狀的

▶ shell [ʃɛl]

【釋】 *n.* 殼

【例】 It takes off the outer *shell* and cleans it.

▶ shiny ['ʃaɪnɪ]

【釋】 *adj.* 有光澤的

【例】 And parts of the morpho butterfly wings are very *shiny*.

【衍】 shine *n.* 光澤 *v.* 閃耀

▶ shut [ʃʌt]

【釋】 *v.* 關閉

【例】 So they sometimes *shut* a small piece of land where there isn't enough food to support them.

【衍】 shutter *n.* 快 門； 百 葉
窗；遮板

【近】 close

▶ sign [saɪn]

【釋】 *n.* 告示

【例】 And then my friend put up
a *sign* in the store saying
that all the jewelry in the
store had been certified as
authentic by a leading ex-
pert.

【衍】 signal *n.* 訊號

▶ significant [sɪgˈnɪfɪkənt]

【釋】 *adj.* 重大的

【例】 And the use of these ma-
chines brought about some
significant changes.

【衍】 significance *n.* 意義；重要性

【近】 important

▶ signpost [ˈsaɪnpost]

【釋】 *n.* 指示牌

【例】 And since the university
doesn't allow us to tie them
to *signposts*, or fences or
anything like that to park
them, I always have to lock
mine up in another building
and walk over to the dining
hall cause there's hardly
ever a space.

▶ silk [sɪlk]

【釋】 *adj.* 絲綢的

【例】 For example, the ancient
Romans never had *silk* fabric.

【衍】 silky *adj.* 絲的；柔滑的

▶ sincerely [sɪn'sɪrlɪ]

【釋】 *adv.* 真誠地

【例】 I *sincerely* respect them all.

【衍】 sincere *adj.* 真誠的

【近】 honestly

▶ single ['sɪŋgl]

【釋】 *adj.* 單一的

【例】 I request a *single* room.

▶ sink [sɪŋk]

【釋】 *v.* 淹沒

【例】 The bottom of the ocean is where archaeologists found an ancient ship that had *sunk*...

【衍】 sinking *adj.* 下沉的

▶ site [saɪt]

【釋】 *n.* 地點

【例】 But there is still some discharge on the drainage *site*.

【近】 location

▶ situation [ˌsɪtʃu'eʃən]

【釋】 *n.* 情況

【例】 I reinterpreted my *situation*.

【近】 circumstance

▶ skyscraper ['skaɪˌskrepɚ]

【釋】 *n.* 摩天大樓

【例】 There were lots of buildings, tall ones, *skyscrapers*, and the cars and signs on the city streets looked old fashioned, like they were from the past, like the 1940s.

▶ slightly ['slaɪtlɪ]

【釋】 *adv.* 略微地

【例】 Now, like I said, there were two groups and each group saw a *slightly* different version of the picture.

▶ sling [slɪŋ]

【釋】 *v.* 吊起

【例】 Put it into its carrying case, and *sling* it over his shoulder.

▶ slip [slɪp]

【釋】 *v.* 滑倒

【例】 When it rains, the dirt turns to mud and becomes very slippery, so the runners who use them can *slip* and fall.

【衍】 slippy *adj.* 光滑的

【近】 slide

▶ slither ['slɪðɚ]

【釋】 *v.* 滑動

【例】 Just *slither* away.

【衍】 slithery *adj.* 滑溜的

【近】 slide, slip

▶ slope [slop]

【釋】 *n.* 斜坡

【例】 The mountain *slopes* can be very steep and rocky.

▶ slot [slɑt]

【釋】 *n.* 位置

【例】 I tried to make a reservation to practice before the winter concert, but I couldn't, because other people from

the orchestra had already
booked every single time
slot.

【近】 location

▶ smooth [smuð]

【釋】 *adj.* 光滑的

【例】 A rough texture can evoke
stronger emotions and
strength while a *smooth*
texture is more calming and
less emotional.

【衍】 smoothly *adv.* 平 穩 地；
流暢地

▶ snack [snæk]

【釋】 *n.* 零食

【例】 A lot of students eat at the
snack bar, or off campus.

▶ snake [snek]

【釋】 *n.* 蛇

【例】 Neither snake ever tried to
injure the other *snake*.

【衍】 snaky *adj.* 陰險的；彎彎
曲曲的

▶ snail [snel]

【釋】 *n.* 蝸牛

【例】 Now, as you know, a *snail*
is a very small creature.

▶ sneaker ['snikɚ]

【釋】 *n.* 運動鞋

【例】 And they all liked to dress
really casually, in T-shirts
and jeans and *sneakers*.

【衍】 sneaky *adj.* 鬼鬼祟祟的；
卑鄙的

▶ **snowstorm** [ˈsnostɔrm]

【釋】 *n.* 暴風雪

【例】 Yeah, I remember that we had a bunch of *snowstorms* in a row last year.

▶ **soccer** [ˈsɑkɚ]

【釋】 *n.* 足球

【例】 I just finished at the Student Medical Center—I twisted my ankle playing *soccer* this morning.

▶ **socialize** [ˈsoʃəlaɪz]

【釋】 *v.* 交際

【例】 Coffeehouses are great, if people actually use them, like to *socialize* with friends, while enjoying a cup of coffee and a snack.

【衍】 social *adj.* 社會的

▶ **sociologist** [ˌsosɪˈɑlədʒɪst]

【釋】 *n.* 社會學家

【例】 I was pretty sure I wanted to be a *sociologist*.

【衍】 social *adj.* 社會的

▶ **softness** [ˈsɔftnɪs]

【釋】 *n.* 柔軟度

【例】 The way an artist paints certain areas of the painting can create the illusion of texture, an object's smoothness or roughness or *softness*.

【衍】 soften *v.* 減輕；使柔和 soft *adj.* 柔軟的

▶ soil [sɔɪl]

【釋】 *n.* 土壤

【例】 Attached to the tree, sometimes 30 or 40 meters high, these aerial plants have access to sunlight but not to nutrients from the *soil* below.

▶ sort [sɔrt]

【釋】 *n.* 種類

【例】 He wanted to buy *sort* of a big house and this house just wasn't that big.

【衍】 sorted *adj.* 分類的

【近】 category

▶ spacious ['speʃəs]

【釋】 *adj.* 寬敞的

【例】 Now the car, the car actually looks kind of small; it's not a big car at all, but you get the sense that it's pretty *spacious*.

【衍】 spaciously *adv.* 寬廣地

【近】 extensive

▶ spaghetti [spə'ɡɛtɪ]

【釋】 *n.* 義大利麵

【例】 Well, I wore my white shirt to dinner and I spilt *spaghetti* sauce all over it.

▶ Spanish ['spænɪʃ]

【釋】 *n.* 西班牙語

【例】 Yeah, but I'm not that excited about taking *Spanish*.

▶ specialize ['spɛʃəlaɪz]

【釋】 *v.* 專業化

【例】 He *specialized* in criminal law.

【衍】 specialized *adj.* 專門的

▶ species ['spiʃiz]

【釋】 *n.* 品種

【例】 There are some *species* of black ants that care for tiny insects called aphids.

▶ spike [spaɪk]

【釋】 *n.* 長釘

【例】 They're like *spikes*, sticking out of the plant that are so numerous and dense that they prevent insects from landing on the leaves.

【衍】 spiked *adj.* 尖的

單字表 8

▶ split [splɪt]

【釋 1】 v. 灑出

【例】 Well, I was just in the cafeteria eating lunch and reading it over one last time when I *split* some soup on it, and the class starts in fifteen minutes.

【釋 2】 *adj.* 爆裂的

【例】 So the shapes were there for a *split* second in dim light and then they were gone.

【衍】 splitting adj. 極快的；爆裂似的

▶ spoon [spun]

【釋】 *n.* 勺子

【例】 It's kind of like digging out a crater with a *spoon* to find a single nugget of gold.

▶ sprain [spren]

【釋】 *v.* 扭傷

【例】 I'm worried I'm gonna be out of practice, like I haven't been able to play the violin since I *sprained* my wrist.

【近】 twist

▶ spray [spreɪ]

【釋】 *v.* 噴射

【例】 The wolf doesn't want to be *sprayed* again, so it backs off and leaves the skunk alone.

【衍】 sprayer *n.* 噴霧器；灑水器

▶ squeeze [skwiz]

【釋】 *n.* 擠壓

【例】 We're all pretty busy but I

think we can *squeeze* in a show before summer starts and everyone goes away.

【衍】 squeezer *n.* 壓榨機；壓榨者

▶ squirrel [skwɝ·əl]

【釋】 *n.* 松鼠

【例】 This squirrel, like many species of *squirrel*, loves to eat nuts.

▶ stable ['stebl]

【釋】 *adj.* 穩定的

【例】 If nothing happens to disrupt or unbalance the relationship between the animal and its habitat, the carrying capacity will remain *stable*.

【衍】 stability *n.* 穩定

【近】 steady

▶ stadium ['stediəm]

【釋】 *n.* 體育場

【例】 But what about the other reason for building the *stadium*? I mean right now we have so little contact with the town.

▶ staff [stæf]

【釋】 *n.* 工作人員

【例】 Instead, students need to request a movie title, and then library *staff* get it for them.

▶ stage [stedʒ]

【釋】 *n.* 舞臺

【例】 And when he first walked out on *stage*, I have to admit, I was a little distracted.

▶ startle ['stɑrtl]

【釋】 *v.* 驚嚇

【例】 Some jellyfish produce bright flashes of light that confuse predators to *startle* them.

【衍】 startling *adj.* 令人吃驚的
startled *adj.* 受驚嚇的

【近】 surprise

▶ statue ['stætʃu]

【釋】 *n.* 雕像

【例】 The next landmark you pass might be the *statue* in front of the library.

【衍】 statuary *adj.* 雕像的

▶ steady ['stɛdɪ]

【釋】 *adj.* 穩定的

【例】 According to a university administrator, the decision was prompted by a *steady* decline in enrollments in evening classes.

【衍】 steadily *adv.* 穩定地；穩固地

【近】 firm

▶ steel [stil]

【釋】 *n.* 鋼鐵

【例】 That, if they start at one end of the bridge and they work to the other end, by the time they finish, it's already time to go back and start painting the beginning of the bridge again, because the bridge was built with steel cables, and *steel* cables can't take the salt air unless they're treated repeatedly with a zinc-based paint.

【衍】 steely *adj.* 鋼 製 的 ； 鋼
鐵般的

▶ stem [stɛm]

【釋】 *n.* 莖

【例】 Its flowers are held on a
single *stem* in the center.

【衍】 stemmed *adj.* 有莖的

▶ stick [stɪk]

【釋】 *v.* 堅持

【例】 They say they're gonna
stick around here during the
break.

【衍】 sticky *adj.* 黏的

▶ sticky ['stɪkɪ]

【釋】 *adj.* 黏的

【例】 Snails secrete a *sticky*,
slimy substance.

【衍】 stick *v.* 堅持 *n.* 棍子

【近】 glutinous

▶ stimulus ['stɪmjələs]

【釋】 *n.* 刺激（複數 stimuli）

【例】 Humans are constantly per-
ceiving visual and auditory
stimuli.

【衍】 stimulation *n.* 刺激；鼓舞

【近】 incentive

▶ stock [stɑk]

【釋】 *n.* 庫存

【例】 No, none of the bookstores
in the campus area had it in
stock.

【衍】 stockholder *n.* 股東

▶ stomach ['stʌmək]

【釋】 *n.* 肚子

【例】 There's a species of eel that has an enormous mouth and a large *stomach* that's capable of expanding.

【衍】 stomachache *n.* 腹痛

【近】 abdomen

▶ straight [stret]

【釋】 *adv.* 直接地

【例】 Other fish are attracted to this light. They think it's something small they can eat, so they swim *straight* toward it.

【衍】 straighten *v.* 變直

【近】 directly

▶ strategy [ˈstrætədʒɪ]

【釋】 *n.* 策略

【例】 In a lot of ads, repetition is a key *strategy*.

【衍】 strategic *adj.* 策略上的

【近】 tactic

▶ strength [strɛŋθ]

【釋】 *n.* 力量

【例】 Require great *strength*, and balance.

【衍】 strengthen *v.* 加強；鞏固

【近】 power

▶ strict [strɪkt]

【釋】 *adj.* 嚴格的

【例】 And professor Adams is *strict* about lateness, too.

【衍】 strictly *adv.* 嚴格地

【近】 rigid

▶ stripe [straɪp]

【釋】 *n.* 條紋

【例】 Their body is mostly black, and they have a big white *stripe* that runs from the top of their head.

【衍】 stripped *adj.* 剝去的

▶ struggle ['strʌgl]

【釋】 *v.* 努力

【例】 Oh, I'm just *struggling* about what to do.

【衍】 struggling *adj.* 奮鬥的

▶ sublimation [ˌsʌblə'meʃən]

【釋】 *n.* 昇華

【例】 Another defense mechanism she might use is what we call, *sublimation*.

▶ subliminal [ˌsʌb'lɪmɪnl]

【釋】 *adj.* 潛在意識的

【例】 Describe what *subliminal* perception is and explain how the experiment discussed by the professor illustrates this phenomenon.

【衍】 subliminally *adv.* 潛意識地

▶ submit [səb'mɪt]

【釋】 *v.* 提交

【例】 You can *submit* it when you return in the fall semester and get your grade then.

【衍】 submission *n.* 投降；提交；服從

▶ substance ['sʌbstəns]

【釋】 *n.* 物質

【例】 But what happens when insects land on sundew's leaves to get the sweet nectar? Well, unfortunately for the insects, the hairs on the leaves also produce a super sticky glue-like *substance*.

【衍】 substantial *adj.* 大量的；實質的

▶ subsurface [sʌb'sɝfɪs]

【釋】 *adj.* 地下的

【例】 Moving around underground is called *subsurface* locomotion.

【近】 underground

▶ subtle ['sʌtl]

【釋】 *adj.* 微妙的

【例】 The way it works is, when an insect is walking nearby on the surface, it produces very *subtle* vibrations in the sand.

【衍】 subtly *adv.* 精細地；巧妙地；敏銳地

【近】 delicate

▶ suburb ['sʌbɝb]

【釋】 *n.* 郊外

【例】 Many students at our university do not live in dormitories. These students live in town or in the *suburbs* and travel to campus every day. The university has decided to provide these commuter students with a special lounge in the student center with couches, chairs, and a television.

▶ summarize ['sʌməˌraɪz]

【釋】 *v.* 總結

【例】 Briefly *summarize* the proposal then state the opinion and the reasons about the proposal.

【衍】 summary *n.* 總結

▶ supervise ['supɚˌvaɪz]

【釋】 *v.* 監督

【例】 Yeah, he's been *supervising* my research on eating behavior in mice.

【衍】 supervision *n.* 監督；管理

▶ surface ['sɝˑfɪs]

【釋】 *n.* 表面

【例】 Because this lizard can move so easily and so quickly underground, it doesn't have to travel on the *surface*, where it would be exposed to dangerously high temperatures.

【近】 face

▶ surrender [sə'rɛndɚ]

【釋】 *v.* 投降

【例】 While each animal attempts to prove its strength in the competition, it typically does so without harming the other animal once the winner is established, that animal gains access to the desired resources, while the weaker animal *surrenders* and leaves the area.

▶ survive [sɚ'vaɪv]

【釋】 *v.* 生存

【例】 These Arctic animals have adapted to the extremely cold temperatures primarily because of certain body features that help them to *survive* in the cold Arctic climate.

【衍】 survival *n.* 生存； 倖存
survivor *n.* 倖存者

▶ suspend [sə'spɛnd]

【釋】 *v.* 暫停

【例】 In fact, every semester we get a few students who've had their borrowing privileges *suspended* completely because they haven't returned books.

【衍】 suspension *n.* 懸浮； 暫停；停職
suspended *adj.* 懸浮的；暫停的

▶ suspension [sə'spɛnʃən]

【釋】 *n.* 暫停

【例】 This ability to temporarily put aside, or suspend, our doubt and believe that the action of a play is real is called the *suspension* of disbelief.

【衍】 suspend *v.* 懸浮； 暫停
suspended *adj.* 懸浮的； 暫停的

▶ swallow ['swɑlo]

【釋】 *v.* 吞

【例】 The insect *swallows* this chemical as it eats.

▶ swarm [swɔrm]

【釋】 *n.* 蜂群

【例】 This complex group behavior is called *swarm* intelligence.

▶ switch [swɪtʃ]

【釋】 v. 變換

【例】 The university will begin *switching* from traditional-bound textbooks to electronic textbooks early next year.

▶ swoop [swup]

【釋】 v. 猛撲

【例】 They spot the mouse and *swoop* down to catch it.

▶ target ['tɑrgɪt]

【釋】 n. 目標

【例】 I'd like to talk to you today about two characteristics of *target* customers that can influence marketing strategy, specifically age and geographic location of *target* customers.

【近】 goal, object

▶ taste [test]

【釋】 v. 嘗出……的味道

【例】 Yeah, really! And the new manager has also added a lot of really healthful foods and snacks, so the food doesn't just *taste* good now.

【衍】 tasteless *adj.* 無味的

▶ tear [tɛr]

【釋】 v. 撕裂

【例】 But I just couldn't give up video games! I was completely *torn*.

【衍】 tearing *adj.* 撕裂的；痛苦的

▶ temperature [tɛmprəˌtʃur]

【釋】 *n.* 溫度

【例】 Then, at night, the *temperature* drops and water inside the crack freezes.

【衍】 temperately *adv.* 適度地；有節制地

▶ tempt [tɛmpt]

【釋】 *v.* 使……感興趣

【例】 Existing consumers might now be *tempted* to switch brands.

【衍】 tempting *adj.* 吸引人的

【近】 attract

▶ thereby [ˌðɛr'baɪ]

【釋】 *adv.* 從而

【例】 More important, removing the bikes would help to fee up space on the racks, *thereby* benefiting people who are actually using their bikes and need places to park them.

▶ threat [θrɛt]

【釋】 *n.* 威脅

【例】 This will be your *threat.*

【衍】 threatened *adj.* 受到威脅的
threatening *adj.* 威脅的

▶ threshold ['θrɛʃhold]

【釋】 *n.* 門檻

【例】 This phenomenon—the perception of a stimulus just below the *threshold* of conscious awareness—is called subliminal perception.

▶ thrive [θraɪv]

【釋】 *v.* 繁榮

【例】 Now, plants, like animals, and like us for that matter, need nutrients, substances that provide nourishment, to survive, *thrive* and grow.

【衍】 thriving *adj.* 繁榮的

【近】 flower

▶ throughout [θru'aut]

【釋】 *prep.* 貫穿

【例】 So, say an insect starts eating a potato plant's leaf, that will cause the plant to react by releasing a chemical *throughout* its leaf system.

▶ thumb [θʌm]

【釋】 *n.* 拇指

【例】 I wasn't being very careful when I smashed my *thumb* with the hammer.

▶ thunder ['θʌndɚ]

【釋】 *n.* 雷

【例】 A giant Australian bird is called the *thunder* bird.

【衍】 thundering *adj.* 如雷鳴的；非常的

▶ tight [taɪt]

【釋】 *adj.* 緊張的

【例】 And my budget is pretty *tight* right now.

【衍】 tightly *adv.* 緊緊地；堅固地

▶ tiny ['taɪnɪ]

【釋】 *adj.* 微小的

【例】 So as the mole goes digging through the dirt with its head push forward, the dirt particles come into contact with the hairy membrane covering the mole's *tiny* eyes.

【衍】 tininess *n.* 極小；微小；單薄

【近】 micro

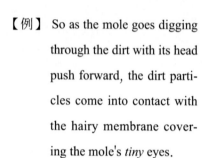

▶ tissue ['tɪʃu]

【釋】 *n.* 組織

【例】 The water is then slowly released from the special bladder into the frog's internal *tissues* until the next rain which might not be for several months.

▶ tomb [tum]

【釋】 *n.* 陵墓

【例】 Besides being built as *tombs*, some of these passage graves were definitely what we might call Astronomical Calendars, with chambers that were flooded with some light on the certain special days of the year, which must've seemed miraculous and inspired a good deal of religious wonder.

▶ ton [tʌn]

【釋】 *n.* 大量

【例】 Besides being closer to work, I'd also save *tons* of money on gas.

▶ tough [tʌf]

【釋】 *adj.* 困難的

【例】 It's gotten really *tough* to find a space.

【衍】 toughly *adv.* 固執地；強硬地

【近】 difficult

▶ trade [tred]

【釋】 *v.* 交易

【例】 In the past, people would only *trade* locally.

【衍】 trader *n.* 交易者

【近】 commerce

▶ traditionally [trə'dɪʃənəlɪ]

【釋】 *adv.* 傳統上

【例】 *Traditionally*, staff members from the admissions office have led the campus tours for secondary-school students who are considering attending the university.

【衍】 traditional *adj.* 傳統的 tradition *n.* 傳統

▶ traffic ['træfɪk]

【釋】 *n.* 交通

【例】 So, there's much more *traffic* now than before.

▶ transition [træn'zɪʃən]

【釋】 *n.* 過渡

【例】 This period of *transition*, when people are adjusting to technological change, is known as cultural lag.

【衍】 transitional *adj.* 變遷的；過渡期的

▶ tutor ['tutɚ]

【釋】 *v.* 輔導

【例】 So you might spend a lot of time *tutoring* him instead of studying the stuff you need to study.

【衍】 tutorial *adj.* 輔導的

▶ type [taɪp]

【釋】 *v.* 打字

【例】 I mean, when I'm at a computer, I'm not just *typing*.

【衍】 typewriter *n.* 打字機

▶ typically [ˈtɪpɪklɪ]

【釋】 *adv.* 通常

【例】 Well, as you say, the media will *typically* focus on only one thing.

【衍】 typical *adj.* 典型的

▶ ultimately [ˈʌltəmɪtlɪ]

【釋】 *adv.* 最終

【例】 *Ultimately,* it will stop responding to the situation altogether.

【衍】 ultimate *adj.* 最終的

【近】 eventually, finally

▶ unconsciously [ʌnˈkɑnʃəslɪ]

【釋】 *adv.* 不知不覺地

【例】 So she'll *unconsciously* find ways to deal with her painful feelings.

【衍】 unconscious *adj.* 無意識的
unconsciousness *n.* 無意識

▶ undercut [ˌʌndɚˈkʌt]

【釋】 *v.* 削弱

【例】 Now this happens when the market is already saturated with the product and the strategy is to *undercut* its competitors.

▶ underground [ˌʌndɚˈɡraʊnd]

【釋】 *adv.* 在地下

【例】 As you may know, rattle-snakes eat various kinds of small animals—small animals that live *underground*, in burrows, in little holes in the ground.

▶ underline [ˈʌndəlaɪn]

【釋】 *v.* 強調

【例】 So what good are all those fancy features if it's hard to use them? Besides, I like the old-fashioned way of studying material: writing notes on the page and *underlining* or highlighting important sections of the book.

【近】 emphasize, stress

▶ unexpected [ˌʌnɪkˈspɛktɪd]

【釋】 *adj.* 意外的

【例】 And we know that when a baby is surprised by something, a loud noise or an *unexpected* flash of light maybe, it stares at where the noise or light is coming from.

【衍】 unexpectedly *adv.* 出乎意料地

【近】 sudden

電子書購買

爽讀 APP

國家圖書館出版品預行編目資料

黃金口說托福 800 單字：從苦背單字到流利口
說對話，托福口說實用單字大公開 / 那天 著 .
-- 第一版 . -- 臺北市：崧燁文化事業有限公司，
2024.05
面； 公分
POD 版
ISBN 978-626-394-247-9(平裝)
1.CST: 托福考試 2.CST: 詞彙
805.1894 113005208

黃金口說托福 800 單字：從苦背單字到流利口說對話，托福口說實用單字大公開

臉書

作　　　者：那天
發 行 人：黃振庭
出 版 者：崧燁文化事業有限公司
發 行 者：崧燁文化事業有限公司
E - m a i l : sonbookservice@gmail.com
粉 絲 頁：https://www.facebook.com/sonbookss/
網　　　址：https://sonbook.net/
地　　　址：台北市中正區重慶南路一段六十一號八樓 815 室
Rm. 815, 8F., No.61, Sec. 1, Chongqing S. Rd., Zhongzheng Dist., Taipei City 100,
Taiwan
電　　　話：(02) 2370-3310　　傳　　　真：(02) 2388-1990
印　　　刷：京峯數位服務有限公司
律師顧問：廣華律師事務所 張珮琦律師

定　　　價：299 元
發行日期：2024 年 05 月第一版
◎本書以 POD 印製